Holiday Word Gifts

Published by Casa de Snapdragon LLC

Library of Congress Cataloging-in-Publication Data
Pending

Published by
Casa de Snapdragon LLC
12901 Bryce Avenue, NE
Albuquerque, NM 87112
http://www.casadesnapdragon.com
20111114

Printed in the United States of America

Holiday words of cheer,
to remember all through the year

A new beginning, another year. Is this a dream, or am I first to take a place along the misty shore on old Gray Pond. If I reach and touch another, and they the same, I will know. This is the day, the world begins, this is the day the world finds peace.
Janet K. Brennan

The woods are lovely, dark, and deep,
But I have promises to keep,
And miles to go before I sleep,
And miles to go before I sleep.
Robert Frost

WISDOM
The best advice my mother gave was to look, listen, and learn.
These three words have given me the ability to evaluate and discern.
Wisdom comes with experiences that have often caused the heart pain.
Of all the things in this world to wish for, wisdom is a great prize to attain.
Happy Holidays - *Kairawan Joseph*

All hail!" the bells of Christmas rang,
"All hail!" the monks at Christmas sang,
The merry monks who kept with cheer
The gladdest day of all their year.
John Greenleaf Whittier

"I lift up mine eyes unto the mountains, from whence cometh my help. My help cometh from the Lord who made heaven and earth. He will not suffer thy foot to be moved. He that keepeth thee will not slumber. He that keepeth Israel doth neither slumber nor sleep. The Lord is thy keeper. The Lord is thy shade upon thy right hand. The sun shall not smite thee by day, nor the moon by night. The Lord shall keep thee from all evil. He shall keep thy soul. The Lord shall guard thy going out and thy coming in, from this time forth and forevermore." Amen.
From *The Diary of Anne Frank*

I dedicate this book to all of the authors and artists around the world who helped make this project possible and to my grandchildren, Erin Elizabeth, Peyton Alexander and Nathan Joseph

The Christmas Tassel

Janet K. Brennan

I saw you standing
a corner deep
of my eye.
There, then gone.
Tall – perfect . . .
jeans and sweater,
hair as spun-gold,
looking toward heaven;
arms raised,
a glory light.

I saw you sitting,
legs wrapped 'round
my piano bench-worn.
You played
a song new, encircled
with webs of grace,
a bridge to another place,
a time lost in space.

I watched you climb through snow,
footprints left behind,
coat, green –hat red,
a Christmas Tassel; and I wonder why
this year
of superfluous joy
I see you and miss you more.

I heard you last night.
Howling secrets through crevices
of waked dreams,
laughter as a brook,
apple mountain soft.
Your voice traveled home
through trans - parent sighs.

Merry Christmas, Mum.
Did you light my candle?
I am here, all ways, I am always here.

Earth Kisses

Michele D'Ambrosio

Emblazoned Earth I am set free
Rebirth at the foothills of my ancestors
Lead me in a sacred dance
Come through me as a mighty change
Cast Your light imprinting visions upon my mind
Renew my fragmented dream
Thus allow me to be cradled in Your nurturing
arms of creativity
Bless the Earth, my home and body with Your
dynamic spirit
Share Your abundance that is mighty like deep
canyons
I know that my tomorrow rests in lucid dreams of
sacred history past
Teach me the language of Love
I perch myself in Your bosom
Oh Great Father Spirit
I am Your offspring
I yield to Thee

The Power of Christmas

Erin Brennan,
Age 11

Sasha awoke with a sharp bark. She had been dreaming a strange dream. It had been about a room full of clocks and bells with Holly, her owner, sleeping at one end, her red hair splayed out on the pillow. Sasha had come bounding over to the bed to wake Holly up, jumping and licking her face. Grinning, she looked at Joe. Joe was her best friend, a border collie.   He did not grin back. Sasha tilted her head. Joe just rolled over and sighed deeply. Sasha panicked. What had just happened? Sasha did not know. Then something amazing happened. There appeared above Joe a dog made of what seemed to be… light? Sasha was startled but she knew what it meant. Joe was going to die. Sasha had to save him. Sasha had been staring at Joe all day. He could not, would not die on her. No way, it was Christmas Eve. Joe was taking a nap when Sasha woke him.

"No naps today, Joe?"

"And why ever not?"

"Do you want to die in your sleep?"

"No, of course not,." Joe replied. He was too sick to argue. "Then no naps." He let it go and decided not to nap. Sasha had her moods. The next day, Joe was sick as a dog. Sasha was worried. It was Christmas, how could Joe be sick? He just wanted to lie down all day.

That night Sasha would not let him go to sleep. Holly put out the fire and went to bed. . Without the fire, it was cold. Sasha drifted off too. That's when Joe heard the knocking at the window. Tap…tap…tap. He looked out and saw a big man with a beard white as snow.

"Hello, Joe," he said. "I have come to help you. Right now you are very sick, but if you sleep tonight when you wake up tomorrow, you will be just fine, as long as you believe in Christmas. "So Joe went to sleep. The next morning Joe woke up before everybody else. Feeling happy and full of energy, he ran around outside. His belly did not hurt any more, and neither did his head. Joe was all better, all thanks to the power of Christmas.

Silent Night on the Mountain

Janet K. Brennan

Patches
lace white from yesterday's flurry,
creep down the mountain
into my heart.

Pillows
ice-gray whisper promise
sent from high places,
leaden with snow.

Winter-Sun-setting
throws fire o'er the mesa,
spreads like a smile
'cross the valley below.

Painting of Grace
could not be more lovely,
as God Himself adds
a brush stroke or two.

Wet hints of snowflakes,
chilled winds from the north,
the finishing touch awaits.
Silent Night.

The finishing touch awaits
Silent Night.

Dusting Cobwebs on a Winter Day

Janet K. Brennan

Scrub Jays clacking secrets,
as shadows of the day trip my mood,
begging gifts of pure release
in my journey through a late daydream.
Palmed feathers chanting of magic
whisper rumors of sun drenched shores,
water babies coming to visit
in a shallow seaweed bay.

Another world, it was!

Made better in the desert chill,
and jack frost mornings of tomorrow.
Burying my toes 'neath feather-down,
remembering. . .
quilts of powder, white laced
with pearly shells and frothy tides
warmed by a tangerine gem
hung low beneath pillows- beige.
Impatient
for that last hurrah into the sea.
Rose and blue tints remain,
melting across a dusky sky.
Creation at its best!
Leaving one thankful tear,
I remember and dream.

While winter birds sing through the night,
and snow hugs old watermelon high.
Winds skip through the canyon and sigh,
sweet dreams, my friend, sweet dreams.

Friends of Montecchia[1]

Janet K. Brennan

"Oh no," I sobbed. "Will I ever survive living in this strange and far away country?" Everything about it was foreign, and all I could think of was, "I want to go home!"

We arrived in Verona, Italy ten days before Christmas. The Santa Lucia Festival at Piazza Brá was in full swing. Vendors from all over Europe had stands and sold their precious gifts and hand-made wares to the visitors as they meandered through the park and through the well-lit coliseum.

We lost a daughter two years prior to asthma, and the family was still in the midst of grieving when military orders arrived for my husband, Arthur. They were sending us to Verona in the Veneto region of Italy. I had lived in foreign countries before, yet this was very different. This tour of duty included no military housing, co-workers, or friends living nearby with which to communicate. We were the only Americans within a twenty-five mile radius. No one in the tiny village of Montecchia di Crosara, where our villa was located, could speak English.

My children, Katie and Nicholas, took the train from the nearby village of San Bonafacio to school each day. Nicholas went west to his school in Verona, and Katie caught the eastbound train to the city of Vicenza, where her high school was located. Art's job took him fifty miles to a tiny World War II village and 2 kilometers deep into a mountain. He drove there in a tiny Fiat. The fog was sometimes as thick as Pea Soup! Meanwhile, I stayed home in our villa for long hours each day and, more often than not, my family did not return until eight o'clock at night. We felt isolated in every sense of the word. Looking at this new assignment as a great learning experience seemed like an insurmountable task. Because of the stress of attempting to heal and return as an intact family after tragedy, we were most definitely, a family in crisis. A hardship assignment to medieval Italy was the last thing in the world we thought we needed.

Many say they envied our situation. Montecchia di Crosara is an ancient village in the Soave province, nestled in the Val d'Alpone. It is surrounded by glorious vineyards, which produce both the red and green grapes that are used to make the delectable Soave wines. In the distance, snowcapped Alps ringed this Veneto area and the village enjoyed a mountain topped by a huge, wooden cross that seemed to stand guard over Montecchia di Crosara.

We would need to adjust. We knew this. We would need to learn the language and mingle as much as possible with our neighbors. This proved difficult as our Italian neighbors were as intimated by us as we were by them.

We had only been in our villa a few days when our Landlord, Signor Marcello Manubosco, arrived at our door with his family. Introductions were made and, before long, we came to feel very much at home with the Manubosco family. They brought huge bundles of firewood for the cold winter that lay ahead of us, and aptly demonstrated the art of baking Pizza over an open hearth. They invited us to their home to enjoy their fine hospitality and sipping delicious wine which they produced themselves from their vineyards.

In the spring, the Signore and his son, Giuseppe, plowed the area beside our home to make way for a garden. Both my husband and son knew nothing about working the land. Fortunately, Giuseppe was kind enough to get them started. He showed them which vegetables did well in the

---

[1] *Friends of Montecchia* was previously published in "Different Worlds, a Virtual Journey, Cyberwit Publications, 2007

rich, Italian soil, which had been farmed for centuries. Before long, vegetables were sprouting up from the ground and, as our village neighbors passed by on their evening strolls, they would stop to inspect the *American Garden.* "Bravo! Bravo!" they would shout. My husband and son were really proud and working in the garden turned out to be very therapeutic. They spent long hours talking and working.

"A garden is more than just putting seeds into the ground," Signore Manubosco would tell us in Italian. "It also produces food for the soul."

How right he was! We soon came to understand why every family in the village spent long hours with their hands buried in the dirt of their own gardens.

Giuseppe often brought friends and relatives to our home, and our children soon began to meet the Italian children of the village. They were interested in learning how Americans played. Nicholas taught them the fine points of baseball, while they taught him the game of soccer. Katie spent afternoons on the front piazza, giggling with the Italian girls and exchanging fashion ideas.

In the fall, the harvest of the grapes began. The Manubosco family invited us to join their family, cousins and all, to partake in picking the luscious fruit from the tender vines. They taught us to drink the natural juice from the grapes as we picked them so that we would not get thirsty and demonstrated the importance of singing while working. One could not work without at least one good tenor amongst them. Often, if we were away for the day running errands, we would come home to find a huge basket of grapes sitting just outside the door. It was wonderful to know that even when we were not out with them working in the vineyards, they were thinking of us.

Once again, Christmas arrived and the tiny village celebrated much in the same style as Verona had done the year before. The castle on the hill was decorated with tiny white lights and the cross on the hill, which seemed to stand guard over the little village, was ablaze. We were proud to place our beautiful Yuletide tree in the front window for all to see as the villagers walked by our home with great curiosity.

It did not take long before we forgot that we were a family in mourning. We were learning how to live again. We had become so busy with the challenge that our hearts and souls forgot to cry. What we thought would be an impossible and sad experience suddenly became joyful, as we watched these beautiful villagers farm their land and harvest their grapes. We learned to dance with them at their festivals and sing with them in their fields.

Needless to say, we will never forget the kindness of our wonderful Italian friends We are a lucky family, who learned the true meaning of friendship and love, and how easily it can transcend any cultural barriers.

We lived in Montecchia di Crosara for two years, all the while learning and growing as a family in a wonderful cultural exchange with our Italian neighbors. When we left that beautiful and ancient village, we felt secure in the knowledge that what we were taking with us, as well as what we were leaving behind, were memories of the richest sort. Oh, yes. Nick also left his baseball glove, Katie her teen magazines, Art his Fiat, and I, of course . . . left my heart.

Rooftops and War

Rainer Ochs Pasca
Age 5

I am a sometimes not listening boy.
I wonder if I could go for a piggyback ride.
I hear noises from rooftops.
I see chimneys that bring snacks.
I want some carrots.
I am a sometimes not listening boy.

I understand that Frosty is not real.
I say that God is real.
I dream of being on rooftops.
I try to play the piano the right way.
I hope there will be no war someday.
I am a sometimes not listening boy.

I pretend to be other people.
I feel nightmares.
I touch a dream.
I worry about bad people who are not real.
I cry when I'm lost.
I am a sometimes not listening boy.

Peace on Earth

On Any Given Christmas

Janet K. Brennan

Life in the tangled space of Natalie Downey was not always easy. She had her piano, an old upright handed down to her from Grammy Downey. This wonderful gift was given to her at the age of ten. Her first accomplished masterpiece was Beethoven's *Moonlight Sonata*. She learned it frame by frame until she could play it in her sleep. Mother would sit in the kitchen by the warm oven and sigh each time Natalie played a wrong note. A wrong note would be accompanied by a sharp slam of her fist on the piano keys causing a cacophony of sound that filled the small apartment they lived in on Newberry Street in the Back Bay of Boston. A tiny, quaint boutique was on the first floor and held a prominent position in the old brownstone. Methodically, she would begin at the very first note until it was perfect, a somewhat difficult feat with this particular song. It seemed as if her life was just a fraction away from this masterpiece in its own complicated rhythm.

"Play *Deck the Halls*, Natalie. You know that's my favorite Christmas song," her mother called from her warm place in the kitchen. "Moonlight Sonata is just so dreary for this happy season."

This was definitely not a yuletide piece of grace for Natalie. Turning sixteen the week before Halloween had not been easy, not when she knew there would be no sweet sixteen Hershey kisses in her pumpkin or junior prom in the spring. No one seemed to want to date a girl who constantly had to wear a scarf on her head to hide the fact that the chemicals had stolen her hair the year before. It was impossible to imagine a sweet boy kissing her puffed out, chipmunk cheeks, the result of steroids that had to be constantly pumped through her veins. Most days she felt all right, and she had her life; that was the important thing. She had been saved from the ravages of leukemia, and a good wish and quick prayer on any given day would keep her that way. People did not die from the disease, that is what they told her at the hospital, and she could be thankful that she had not contracted this mysterious disease twenty years ago. All of this made perfect sense to Natalie. Yes, she truly was happy that she was alive and not born twenty years ago . . . she guessed. So why did she prefer *Moonlight Sonata* to *Deck the Halls?*

"You need an attitude adjustment," her father said as he deposited the Boston Globe onto the floor. "You're a lucky girl, Nat. You stared death in the eye and knocked it flat on its face."

But to sixteen year old Natalie Downey, it didn't seem that way. It was more like, *You stared death in the face and said "wait a minute.'* The jury was out. It could come back on any given day, and she could be looking at the same disease all over again. Didn't her parents realize that? She knew that they did. Although they didn't realize it, most nights before falling to dreams, Natalie often heard their quiet conversations through the heater vent in her bedroom.

Natalie began her chemotherapy immediately after diagnosis and, within three months, she lost her beautiful, long, dark, Grammy Downey curls. "We can go the wig route, honey, or you can wear a hat or scarf. It is up to you. Beauty is not on the surface, it's what's inside that matters and maybe it's time for you to show just what a gorgeous gal you really are." Wow, something in this entire madness was actually *up to her*. She loved the sound of those words, just knowing that she could make a decision about her own life at a time when it seemed as if her own life was in someone else's hands. They went the wig route and searched catalogs, brochures and clinics for just the right style and size. There were agencies that offered to donate human hair for her, but Natalie settled on a deep-brown, curly wig that resembled her own hair. They were careful to purchase it just as her hair began to thin and lose its shine. No one would ever know. It was not until one blustery day, a few days before Thanksgiving, as Natalie was going between junior geometry and economics, the wind kicked up between buildings and the wig took off like a wayward sea gull. It landed behind the physical education building, just off campus. Well, for heaven's sake, why was the decision of wig or no wig given to her in the first place when the matter was settled by a quick act of nature and God. God, in His infinite mercy, or lack thereof to her way of thinking, had made the decision for her. She had never been impressed with His sense of humor and she was not about to change her mind.

"Not to worry, dear," said Natalie's mother, "I always felt that the best thing to do was to let your friends see your true self shining through your eyes with a lovely little scarf to compliment your Grammy Downey's unique shade of green that I always see staring back at me when I look at you." Before long, Natalie's mother heard the tinkling sound of the first bars of *Moonlight Sonata* emanating from the family room. *Oh dear, that told her everything!*

The week leading up to Christmas day finally arrived in Boston. The lights, which were strung at Thanksgiving on Commonwealth Avenue, swayed in the city wind that seemed to claim its way through the tiny alleys and down the narrow streets. Natalie did not feel well. She was careful to take her medicine every day, and mother and father had set up a home movie system in the den so that she could stay on top of the latest movies without going to the theater. School was still in her every day schedule, and the colds and flu of the season had eventually made their way into the classrooms of St Joseph School for Girls. Just two days before Christmas, Natalie was running a high fever and into the hospital she went. "Quarantine" said old Doc Murphy. "No one but your parents can visit, and they will need to disinfect before going into the room. Your temperature is dangerously high and we need to get it down and get rid of whatever infection has hit you this time. You know, Natalie, your resistance is next to zero. You are neutrapenic. That means that you are susceptible to just about any kind of vile bacteria that you are exposed to."

"I know, I know, Doctor Murphy," said Natalie as she weakly fluffed her hospital pillow into a comfortable position and settled in for what would be a very long nap. When she awoke, she saw her mother sleeping in the corner chair. Her father had gone home for the night. Glancing at the wall clock, she saw that she had been sleeping for hours. It was four a.m. and tonight was Christmas Eve. Her body was drenched in sweat and her fever had broken sometime during the sleep. Crawling from her bed, she quietly opened her hospital door to head down to the nurse's station for some dry gowns.

"Hello," said a tiny voice from the room across the hall. Natalie stopped short and glanced inside the pristine room. A little girl sat on the edge of her bed. "I'm like you, see? I have no hair, either. We are the same, except of course, you are much more beautiful and older. I can't wait until I am a teenager like you!"

Natalie entered the room and sat on a near chair. "You have cancer, too?"

"Oh yes," said the little girl. "I was diagnosed when I was five. I'm supposed to be in remission, but I keep getting colds and have to come back here for a stay. Now I'm six. My name is Sonya Garcia, but you can call me Sunny, everyone does."

Natalie felt her heart break at that moment. *My God, she was only six!*

"Well, pleased to meet you, Sunny. Yes, I'm older. I'm a junior in high school this year."

Sunny's eyes grew wide. "Wow, my sister, Miriam, is a junior this year too. She's going to go to her Junior Prom in the spring. Will you be going?"

Natalie shook her head. "I doubt it, who would want to take me to the Prom looking like I do."

Sunny giggled. "Why, everyone! You are so beautiful. I'll bet you have a special talent, too. Mine is my voice. I sing like an opera singer. I never could, but suddenly a few months ago, there it was. Everyone was so surprised. My Mommy said it was a direct gift from God after I got cancer . . . to help make things better for me and give me something else to think about. I'm going to be a rock star when I grow up." Natalie laughed. "Yes, I play piano, but I'll be lucky if I get through my first recital this year," she said. Sunny frowned "Oh you must! Can you play Miley Cyrus songs? My favorite Christmas song is *Deck the Halls*, can you play *Deck the Halls*?"

"No, but I can play Beethoven's *Moonlight Sonata*." Mother doesn't like it much; she likes *Deck the Halls*, like you do. She thinks *Moonlight Sonata* is just too somber, especially for this time of year."

Sunny got up from her bed and threw her arms around Natalie. "I'm so happy to have a friend here with me this Christmas. Mommy says Santa will come here to my hospital room and I'll bet he'll go to yours, too." Sunny unwrapped a bright blue scarf from her head and held it out to Natalie. "Here, it's yours, my gift to you. We really can't expect Santa to remember that we don't have hair, and that color looks so beautiful on you." Sunny yawned and curled into the corner of her bed. "I'll see you in the morning, but now the nurse says I have to get to sleep."

"Well, Sunny. I may not be here. My fever broke and, once that happens, they usually send me home to recover, especially since it's Christmas."

Sunny sighed. "Well, I wish you could be here with me, but I'll say a prayer to Jesus that you can go home and be with your family. That really would be the very best!"

Natalie stood to leave and helped tuck Sunny back into her bed. "I'll check on you tomorrow morning and we can have a fun visit." She retrieved a dry hospital gown from the cart outside her door, entered her room and changed into it. Mother was still asleep, and Natalie quietly slipped beneath the covers of her bed and fell asleep for the night. When morning arrived and Natalie opened her eyes, she was pleased to find both her mother and Doctor Murphy leaning over her. She was dry and she felt better. "Your fever broke during the night, Natalie," said Doctor Murphy. "We'll run some tests and let you go sometime this afternoon if things stay good."

As soon as the doctor left the room, Natalie's mother began to pack up her things and place them in the small backpack. Natalie's thoughts ran immediately to Sunny across the hall. "I'll be right back, Mother. I met a little girl last night, only six years old. She's in the room across the hall and I want to say good-bye to her."

Natalie quietly opened the door. Maybe Sunny was still asleep. To her surprise, the room was empty and the bed stripped of its linens. *Where was the little girl?* Just as Natalie was about to turn down the hall, the morning nurse greeted her with a smile. "What is it, Nat? You look puzzled."

"Well, I went to visit the little girl, Sunny, this morning and she was gone. Did she go home"?

The nurse took a step back and looked deeply into Natalie's eyes. "Sweetheart, there was no little girl in that room. It's been empty for quite some time. Actually, we've been using it for storage until the new ward is up and running."

"But you must be mistaken," said Natalie. "I visited her for quite a while last night. She was there and we laughed and sang and . . . . "

Natalie's mother took her arm. "Let's go Nat, the day awaits. Family will be at the house."

"How strange," thought Natalie. Well, she would get to the bottom of that one.

"Natalie," called the morning nurse. "You aren't the first one to meet our Sunny. Many young people have gone into that room, especially during the holiday season, and met a little girl who sounds just like your little girl. We think she was Saundra Wilson, a little cancer patient that we lost a few years ago. I can't say that I have ever seen her or that I believe in spirits, but this does make me wonder since so many children have seen her."

Natalie's mother smiled. "It was most likely a dream. You slept pretty soundly last night, honey. When a fever is about to break, we sometimes have strange dreams."

Natalie was adamant. "No, Mother, I went into her room and I met her. I know a dream from reality."

~~~

Christmas was lovely that year, and Natalie found herself thinking often about her little friend. "Mistakes are made all the time, Nat," said her father. "But I don't think the staff would misplace a patient. It was just a dream. Maybe the little spirit visited you in your dream, not that I think that is likely, and I doubt that you do either. You are far too practical a young lady to believe in ghosts. But, who knows? I've heard stranger things, especially during the holiday season." Natalie agreed, she supposed it was possible.

The holiday season was glorious that year. Natalie learned to play *Deck the Halls* for her mother and, by New Years, albeit late for Christmas, Natalie played her mother's favorite song on the piano.

"What will you play for recital this year, Hon? It's time to start thinking about that. Do you think you will go with *Moonlight Sonata*?"

"Oh, no, Mother. I know it sounds crazy, but I am thinking about *Anitra's Dance*. It's lively and fun with just a few bars from *Deck the Halls* thrown in for good measure and good luck. The song has such new meaning for me now."

"And a new wig, have you made up your mind to that?"

Natalie sighed. "I won't have it fall off during a moment of wild frenzy while I'm going up and down the scale in *Anitra's Dance!*" They both laughed at the sight it brought to mind.

"Mother, when I unpacked my back pack from the hospital, I couldn't find the blue scarf. Have you seen it?"

Natalie's mother shook her head. "No, Nat. I washed everything and there was no blue scarf. I don't remember you ever having a blue scarf, you like pink."

Natalie frowned. Perhaps it was all just a dream. Well, she would wear her pink scarf as she always did. It would bring her the luck she so longed to have. Was beauty truly deep inside a person? That remained to be seen and, since one could not actually see what was inside a person without x-rays, the answer to that question would remain a mystery. She didn't feel beautiful, inside or out. She could remember a time when she felt healthy and filled with energy, but as her disease took hold, she grew more and more exhausted until that day she fell to the floor in pain and was rushed to the hospital. After that, nothing was normal in her life again; nothing but her love for music and the piano, and they served her well!

The night was blustery and winter-cold in Boston. Leftover Christmas snow seemed to seep from the cracks in the sidewalk, and the snow banks made by the city plow during the previous week's storm were grey and dusty. The cold wind off the harbor bit at her bare legs as she and her parents walked quickly to the library across from Park Square, where she would give her recital. People were gathered out front, programs in hand, waiting for the doors to open. Once inside, Natalie opened her music to the page she needed and stretched her fingers. As the lights dimmed, she knew this was her queue for the start of the program. A jangle of nerves set her body on edge but
~~~

quickly dissipated as they called her name and she walked out on to the stage. Silence reigned over the small library theater and she began playing. Every note resonated to the high rafters and out through to the audience. When she was finished, she stood, made a quick bow to a thunderous applause, and exited to the back stage area where she found her mother, tears brimming. She was holding a single stem rose for Natalie.

"Beautiful, Nat, just beautiful," she proclaimed.

"Yes," came the sound of two voices in unison. "Natalie, you play so wonderfully. I'm so proud that you're my new friend!" As she turned toward the sound of the voice, she was surprised to see a little girl with a broad smile that reminded her of the one she had fallen in love with on Christmas Eve in the Hospital. "Remember me? I'm Sunny!"

Why, it *was* Sunny, after all. Her miraculous little angel Sunny was standing there with her older sister, Miriam.

"Sunny told me you would be playing here tonight, Natalie. She wanted to come and be a part of your recital." Sunny stepped forward and handed Natalie the blue scarf she had given her in the hospital. "I think you dropped it, Natalie, so I saved it for you."

"Wow, miracles *do* happen," declared Natalie, "wonderful, happy miracles!" She hugged her new little friend, holding her close to her. "I thought . . . well, they thought . . . well, never mind. I'm just so happy to see you. Come home with us and have something to eat. How are you feeling?"

Sunny beamed "I'm still in remission, Natalie, and I'm going to stay that way. I'm going to grow up and be just as beautiful as you, and be a rock star and sing on stage, just like you play piano on stage."

Natalie laughed. "I bet you will, Sunny, and I'm going to go to the spring prom. I will never forget this Christmas."

~

The night was cold and wintery as the winds from the River Seine spread across the city of Paris. Tonight would be glorious! The theater across the square from the Place de l'Opera was bright, and the doors were opened to welcome the guests and fans of Natalie Downey. It was Christmas in the City of Lights, and tiny white diamonds sprinkled the bridges that crossed to the West Bank, as well as along the Champs Elyse.

They would meet at the back door stage entrance and walk into the theater as planned, hand in hand.

"Oh, how lovely to see you," beamed the women standing in the dim light of the back stage door. "The house is filled tonight, and here we are, you and me, together. I have my music ready, and I'm certain that you do too, Natalie. Let's go entertain on this happy and beautiful Christmas." Natalie Downey and the famous Sonya Garcia walked briskly through the dressing area, past the back portals of the old theater and on to the stage.

Angels Among Us

Sarah Wilson

Quilt done by Sarah Wilson

Holiday clouds rise soft and solid,
tower in effervescent mist. It is cold.
This bailiwick, a finger hole, in a holiday
cosmos spreads milky.

Here we shimmy wicked lands,
dance in psychedelic realms,
turn the mind to snow.
Eyes close and dream
of uncomplicated things,
inhale the atmospheric stir,
search for black holes, and fly
above the precipitous mountain.

The sky is a forest, gorges narrow.
I shape change to a peacock thin,
and quick, cover land like feathered
rainbow that opens and closes,
but cannot move from side to side,
then shift to a Priest Tree

meditating on thoughts
old as earth itself.

Moonlight feeds blooming white.
Thorns, prickles and spikes crop,
crooked as mandrake root
take on new magical meanings.

Pine trees twirl crystal trunks,
reflect light like mirrors,
and turn holidays into stiff mazes.

Distant stars become hanging bulbs,
butterfly-monkeys, strange swan-horses,
and a twinkly child's eye.

Constant movement skims the sky pool,
where the dead follow this path.

Deer skirmish fast toward three heavens,
often in threes, and chase the dark, as do I.

Evergreens fragrance air, and I'm human again.

Scenery hangs highways in the sky,
winds upward, sideways,
pronounces mist round barns.

The gaze forms gorges.
Rocks cluster, flowers a poinsettia dusk.
Veiled fingers tap clock hands forward,
and sunset lingers.
Orange disk repaints land,
yesterday sea green,
today chocolate,
tomorrow white,
perhaps a carnival view.

Countryside shimmers like burning ethanol,
and I'm upside down, happy to be lost
in a holiday wish that would wrap up
all the good memories, tie them in bows,
and a box I could give to you any day
of the year.

The Little Shop on Piazza Erbe

Janet K. Brennan

"Lira, per favore, Signora? Lira?" Sasha Trembley turned to watch a woman carrying her little baby, sleeping soundly and bundled in deep, rich wool. It was unseasonably cold for the month of December in Verona, Italy. Two weeks before Christmas usually boasted some of the nicest weather of the year, however this year the Veronese climate had taken a turn, which often included pea soup fog and a slight drizzle. Sasha awakened early that morning to prepare for a day of shopping along the Piazza Erbe where the stores, boutiques, and leather markets all flashed their goods in the store windows. They were beautifully rich products. Tiny, white lights adorned the shop entrances as well as lush pine trees. They were decorated with Italian and German wood ornaments and delicate crystal from France. They beckoned to the Veronese shopper to come inside and inhale the soft, warm aroma of burning spice and deep, dark cappuccino, which brewed on burners in the back of the shops. At any other time in her life, this would have been an exciting adventure for Sasha; however, a dark veil of sadness enveloped her entire being, and most days just a smile was impossible.

Sasha's husband, Daniel, and their two children, Laurel and Evan, had arrived in country just a few weeks prior and had settled into the Hotel Castelvecchio until proper accommodations could be found. They needed a small apartment that would suffice until they would return to their home in Vermont. The castle property was a grand place to live with all of its hidden entryways and staircases that creaked and groaned. It sported a two-person lift for the residents who lived on the upper floors of the hotel. The Trembley family had a suite on the top floor, which once was a part of the castle itself.

Daniel Trembley had been asked to move with his family to Italy on a job assignment that would last three years. He welcomed the opportunity, believing that it would be a wonderful and exciting adventure for his family. Best of all it provided a change of scenery. They needed a change. They had lost their eldest daughter, Lisa Marie, to asthma just two years prior. Sasha was not the same woman he had married thirteen years ago. This could be a re-birth for all of them, which would allow them to move on. Nevertheless, Sasha, poor Sasha, seemed to sink even lower into her quagmire of depression after their arrival, and he was at his wit's end. She barely left their hotel and, when she did, she would not enter any of the beautiful churches, shops or ristorantes in the lovely city on the Adige River. "I want you to walk every day, my love," said Daniel. "Just a few blocks. It will help."

Sasha wandered. Was she seeing anything? Did she realize that this was a most incredible city, and that she was being given a chance to heal from the pain of losing a child? It did not seem like it. Most nights after she returned from her walks, she curled up and dozed under the fleece throw on the couch that had *Home Sweet Home* embroidered boldly across the front. The children had begged her to rally and go shopping for a small Christmas tree, however her entire body was sore, and most days she could barely raise her head from her pillow. "Tomorrow night, guys. I promise."

That day, as she rounded the corner, Sasha saw what she thought was the most beautiful little tree she had ever seen. It was decorated with tiny, crystal doves, and fairy white lights sparkled against them, setting them on fire with brilliance. It was set against an outside wall that was part of a little shop. It appeared to be standing guard, albeit timidly.

"Go ahead, Signora, feel free to touch it. It is beautiful, is it not?" Behind her stood an elderly Italian gentleman. Sasha thought he looked like Geppetto from the children's book, "Pinocchio." His voice was soft and kind and Sasha immediately reached out to touch his extended hand.

"Oh, yes. It's the most beautiful tree I have ever seen," said Sasha. "But I don't want to bruise the delicate branches."

He laughed. "This is my shop, lovely American lady, and you have my permission to touch that tree. I brought it down here myself from Cervina."

Holding Sasha's arm gently, the man took her down the steps that led to his shop. They stopped just outside the front door where the glorious little tree stood. It was even more beautiful up close, and she could not resist reaching out to touch its feathered branches. They were soft and the sweet scent of pine invaded her senses.

"You seem very sad, my new friend. Why don't you buy this tree? It will lighten your holidays and bring joy into your life."

Sasha shook her head. "Oh no, I can't. I'm certain that I can't afford it. Save it for the children who will most certainly see it and want their parents to buy it for their Christmas celebration."

The man nodded. "That is very kind of you, but so far, no one has seemed to notice it. I really am eager to sell it. It grows drier each day that it sits out here in the sun. See, even now, there is just a bit of a tilt in the branches. Handing Sasha an old green and rusted watering can, he said, "Per favore, I am an old man. Would you do me the favor of replacing the water in the tree stand? It is dry." Sasha happily poured the clean, fresh water into the stand and could almost see the little tree's branches lift.

"Where are you living, Signora?"

"We are at the Castelvecchio until we can find a suitable apartment not too far from the American compound," said Sasha.

"Oh! That is a beautiful place. You are quite lucky, indeed! Yet you seem very sad."

Sasha sighed. "This will be a sad Christmas, I'm afraid. I lost my oldest child to asthma, last year. I miss her and can't get past the grief, Signore."

Once again, the gentle man took Sasha's hand into his. "But it is Christmas, dear lady, a time for miracles and joy. You cannot save her - she is gone. Now it is time to think about the living."

Sasha shook her head. "Yes, of course, but I can't help but feel that I could have kept her alive if I had just been better about making sure that she took her medicine and breathing treatments . . . perhaps surgery . . . perhaps . . . ." He once again placed the old watering can in her hand. "Take this, you do not live far from here. Every day I would like you to give me some help with this tree. I want you to come here and put fresh water in the tree stand so that it will not perish. You will be doing me a great favor."

Although Sasha declined the offer, he would not listen and, with a quick wave of his hand, he disappeared behind the door of his shop. Sasha hurried back to the hotel, eager to melt into the safe warmth of her fleece *Home Sweet Home* blanket.

The following day, as Sasha dressed, she gazed from her hotel window. Her watering jug was balanced precariously on the side of her bedside table. What could it hurt just this once? The tree was so lovely, and she hated to see it die for lack of care. If she went there every day to water it, some lucky family would be able to enjoy its beauty through the Christmas festivities. What harm could it do?

Upon arriving at the shop, she could see her friend working busily inside with a customer. He waved to her and went back to his business. She felt good. Somehow, she was rejuvenated in a way that she had not felt in a very long time. Yes, she would do her new friend the favor of watering the tree. He couldn't bend or stoop, and she was young. Why not help when she could?

The following day, Sasha arrived at mid-day to care for the tree.

"Hello Signora!" he shouted from inside the shop. "Come in when you are finished. You have done no Christmas shopping for your family. I have some lovely things you might want to see."

At first, Sasha hesitated. She had not been inside a shop in many months and she was not certain whether she would be able to do this. However, when she finished, she set the watering can down on the steps and peered inside the shop. It was filled with gifts of every sort from all around the world, bright and colorful gifts that made Sasha smile. Wooden puppets hung from hooks around the tops of the walls, dressed in lederhosen and green caps with fluffy feathers. Gorgeous, pastel ceramic dolls in pink dresses smiled down at her from the top shelves. Sasha immediately found a pair of wool socks from Zermatt, Switzerland that she knew Daniel would love. On one of the back shelves, she spied a painted truck, large with big round wheels. It would be perfect for Evan. It was hand crafted by an artisan from Bavaria. A porcelain jewelry box from Austria caught her eye. When she opened its lid, the tender song "Edelweiss" filled the lovely, little shop with delicate music. Lauren would just fall in love with this!

"I will take all three of these Signore, per favore."

Sasha went to the little shop every day with her watering can. She pruned dried branches and polished the crystal doves with a soft rag she brought from the hotel. This little activity became the highlight of her day as she walked the streets of Verona and watched the shop windows grow more and more beautiful with holiday decorations and lights as Christmas day approached.

Then, one day, just three days before Christmas, Sasha walked to the shop with one hundred and fifty-three thousand lira, 102 American dollars, in her pocket. Daniel had given it to her only the night before.

"I want you to buy that tree," he said. "You cared for it, you say it's beautiful. We should have it."

She could barely wait to tell the Signore that she was going to be the one to buy the tree after all. However, as she rounded the corner and headed up the little street, she saw that the entryway to the shop was bare and swept clean. The tree was gone! How could this be? It wasn't there! Moreover, the little shop was closed up tight.

Sitting on the top step, Sasha felt she would cry, when she was suddenly interrupted by the voice of a woman who had come up behind her. "Ciao, signora. Are you looking for Signore Bustello?" she asked. "He closed up his shop for the holidays and has gone to Cervina in the north to spend this time with his children. He goes every year. I am Signora Maria, the owner of the leather shop next door. Is there something I can do for you?"

"Oh, no," Sasha sighed. "It's just that I was caring for his little pine tree here in the entry way until he could find someone to buy it for their holiday. Today I thought I might buy it from him."

Signora Maria laughed heartily. "Oh, that sweet little tree. Yes, he gave it to a family just this morning. No one seemed interested in it because it was so small, so he decided to give it away to a very deserving family. He will be back after the New Year rings in and you will find him busy here preparing for Carnavale. I will let him know that you stopped by."

Leaving the watering can by the front door, Sasha slowly walked back to the hotel. This would be an odd Christmas for the family. They would be far from their home in Vermont, no snow, and now, because she had waited so long . . . no Christmas tree. But Daniel had warned that there would be sacrifices they would need to make in order to stay together for this assignment, and this was simply one of them. All the same, it was sad, and Sasha blamed herself for not helping to make the holiday a bit more joyous, especially this year.

Entering the lobby, she was greeted by Luigi, the desk clerk. "Buon Natale, Merry Christmas," he shouted merrily. After taking the lift to the second floor, Sasha headed up the stairs to the fourth floor. Although the door to their flat was locked, she could see through the crack on the side of the old door that lights were on inside. When she unlocked the door, how surprised she was to find Evan, Lauren, and Daniel laughing happily and waiting for her. "What's going on?" she asked.

"Look, Mom . . . a surprise for you!" The three of them moved aside revealing a beautiful little tree lit with sparkling white lights and crystal ornaments on each branch. "Here's your tree, Mom, the one you worked so hard on each day."

Sure enough, there it was! "Oh my!" she exclaimed. "How in the world did you get it?"

Daniel took her hand into his. "Very early this morning, a gentle and kind Signore came by with this tree. He said it was the one that you had cared for and that no one was more deserving than you to have such a Christmas gift."

Sasha was speechless. Walking over to the tree, she touched its branches - soft and delicate. Attached to the very top of the tree was a note. Sasha carefully took it down and unwrapped the envelope.

Dear Sasha,

   Thank you very much for caring for my little friend. Each day you came by, you gave it water and stroked its beautiful, green branches. My hope is that now you will truly know that there is a time and a season for everything in life. And, when the holidays are over and you must plant this tree into the ground, you will always remember how you cared, loved and cherished it for the time you had it with you."

Christmas that year was lovely for the Trembley family. When it was over, they found a beautiful little house on the outskirts of Verona, and they planted Sasha's little tree in a small garden behind the house. As the villagers of this small medieval village tell it, every day Sasha could be seen watering and caring for the tree. She watched it thrive and grow. It remained strong and healthy until the last year the Trembley family lived in Italy. That year the country suffered a severe drought, and many of the beautiful pines in the little village died. Nothing anyone could do would have saved them, and Sasha lost her lovely little tree. Many of the villagers replanted in the same spot and began the cycle of caring for the seedlings. The Trembley family did the same, and then, just before leaving their little village to return to their home in Vermont, Sasha knew . . . . She finally saw just what it was that the kind Signore had been trying to tell her that wintery day when she found her little tree in front of his shop on the Piazza Erbe.

The Last Hunt

Janet K. Brennan

It was Christmas, Nineteen Hundred and Fifty -Eight. We stood in the snowy field, Dad and I. The wind was coming down old White Mountain faster than a runaway locomotive, and I was thankful I had taken my plaid, flap hat with me when we left our cabin on that very early Christmas morning. It was given to me on the previous Christmas by my mother. I had just turned ten, and what I really wanted was a BB gun, however Mum thought otherwise.

"Take your hat, son. You do not want a cold to settle in those ears before the New Year rings in," she warned. Although I despised that silly looking flap hat, I was happy to have it that day. Crossing Weed Pond, Dad and I, with Barney McGee, our Irish Setter, set out for a short hunt just as we did every year on Christmas morning.

"Don't shoot anything more than wild geese, guys. Christmas is a holy day," admonished my mother. Dad winked at me and off we went. We knew that Mum would be home stuffing the turkey and baking mince pie and buttered squash. These delicious thoughts, along with the wonderful Christmas aromas that would greet us when we returned home, kept our souls warm those crisp Christmas mornings when the entire world was still asleep, and our snowshoes crunched the top of layered ice on the frozen pond. It just did not get any better than this. Dad, me, and good old Barney McGee set off for a few hours in the deep woods of New Hampshire. The cold wind would turn our noses brighter than Rudolph's had been only the night before!

I could not help but notice that Dad was a bit slower that Christmas. He seemed to favor his right leg and he didn't hold his Winchester quite as firmly as he always did. "Just getting old, son, just getting old!"

We hadn't gone far out on the pond when we heard it. Dad stopped in his tracks. "What in Sam Hill was that?" he asked. There it was again. Not a howl, not a growl, but a sound that caused the blood in our veins to curdle. Barney stiffened and pointed just as he always did when we were on the hunt. There was something in the woods at the clearing and it was watching us.

"Son, I do not know what that is, but get ready because I think it is going to charge us."

That would have been unusual. Most animals around Weed Pond knew who we were. Not that we were a formidable threesome, it was just a tradition for us to hunt on Christmas morning, and the wild life that made their homes around our log cabin seemed to know that.

As we approached the other side of the pond, we could see something very large and dark burrowing deep into the snow and watching our every move.

"Dang!" said Dad. "Well, son, that is probably the largest black bear I have ever seen around these parts. Look at her eyes, she is ornery. We may be getting too close to a cub. Better for us to back off and head off across the pond in the other direction, toward Grahams Mill. We need to let this one alone!"

However, no sooner had the words been uttered when the bear leapt to her feet and began a charge so fast that we didn't have time to move. Dad was a bit slower than I was and bore the brunt of the attack. Barney flew into the air and attacked from behind, but it was too little too late. Dad was caught within the grips of the bear who wrestled him to the ground, throwing her weight on top of him.

"Help! Help!" I called. The bear caught my Dad … the bear caught my Dad!"

To my surprise, she didn't move. She didn't drag him off, nor did she maul him. Dad was bleeding from a small gash on the side of his face due to his fall. I did notice that he was having difficulty breathing because of the intense weight of the animal who seemed content to keep him beneath her. Barney barked and growled, but the black bear paid no attention. She seemed to hear him, yet only issued a soft growl in return. It was then that I noticed the trail of blood she had left behind her when she had dashed for us from the shore. "She's injured, Barney. This bear is bleeding and hurt. Looks like she ran into a trap or the trap ran into her." No sooner had I said those words than the black bear raised her huge head and growled so loud the sound echoed off the bare, frozen pond and into the woods on the other side of us.

"She's going to keep him there, Barney. She won't release him until we get help."

Horrified by the thought of leaving my dad there and not knowing what we would come back to find, I hesitated. This bear could suddenly change her mind and attack for food. But something had to be done.

Taking a few steps back, I noticed that my dad had become unconscious and his breathing grew shallower by the minute. With a quick leap and bound across the ice, I quickly headed back to our cabin, calling after my setter. He was not following, nor was he ahead of me. When I stopped quickly to see where he was, I saw that Barney McGee was back with Dad and the bear. He would not leave their side.

"Mum, Mum!" I called as I headed north to our cabin. She was just putting the pies out on the railing of our front porch to cool in the crisp mountain air. Throwing down her apron, she knew immediately that something was wrong.

"It's Dad. A black bear has him on the ice. She has him pinned under her. She is bleeding and very hurt. We need to get the rangers out there. We can't do this by ourselves."

Mum wasted no time. Within minutes, two large Fleetsides piled high with rifles and nets approached the cabin. Dan Thomson from Grahams Mill leapt from one of the trucks and breathlessly hollered. "Let's go, Son. We can be there in minutes. We'll have to shoot the bear, I'm sure, but if she's wounded already, it will probably be a good thing. We'll get your dad. Don't worry."

Off we sped toward the pond hoping and praying that Barney McGee had kept the situation from evolving into a tragedy. Leaving the trucks on the far side of the pond so that the sound of the engines would not frighten the bear, we made the remainder of the trek on foot. As we got closer, we couldn't see Barney.

"Where's my dog? "I cried. "I don't see my dog!"

As I cried these words, I could hear the sound of his bark and knew that he had been there all along. Barney had thrown his body on top of the bear's body. What a sight! My dad on the bottom, old black bear in the middle, and Barney McGee on top. There was a silence that fell among us as we watched the surprising scene.

"Don't shoot her!" I cried. "She could have killed my father but she did not. She wants us to help her. I think Barney is telling us that he wants to save everyone here. He's trying to keep everyone warm. We need to save the bear if we can."

"But you guys were hunting," came the response from the rangers.

"Yes, but we don't take our kill this way," I said adamantly. We quickly netted the motionless bear. It took ten of us to pull her off my dad and drag her to the other side of the pond. There she was tranquilized and finally moved to the flat bed of the Fleetside. It sped off to the Ranger's station at Graham's Mill. Dad was just beginning to regain consciousness and moaned.

"You're all right, Dad. Barney here kept you warm and you kept the bear warm."

That was what she wanted. That and to be cared for. When we loaded her into Sam's pick-up, we noticed a cub peeking at us from behind a nearby pine tree. It appeared to be frightened and in shock. "You are very lucky, Dad," I said, trying to comfort my father as he shook from the cold. "That huge bear could have killed you if she had wanted to. Other than a scratch on your face and a torn up jacket and … and … my missing flap hat, I would say you are one lucky guy. Old black bear gave you a great Christmas present and it would seem that you did the same for her!" And she had given me one, as well. At some point during the attack, the wind had taken my flap hat and carried it clear across the ice to the other side of the pond.

That night, after the fire had grown low and the embers popped about in the chimney, I set my mind to thinking. I loved Christmas and this year, although we had a fright and near tragedy, it had all turned out well and would prove to be a forever memory in our family. Mum's dinner tasted especially grand that year and Dad's moan of pure pleasure as he slipped beneath the warmth of his quilts for bed with Barney McGee at his feet, was music to my ears. It was far better than any rendition of *Deck the Halls*. That was certain.

Not long into January, we learned that the black bear's injuries had been cared for and, although it took some time, she was returned to the wild near her cub. We knew that she was never very far from our cabin. Sometimes in the late evening, we heard what sounded like a big old black bear tromping around our back property, snorting and chomping on dried pinecones from the autumn drop. It was not until my old flap hat, with one flap missing, mysteriously appeared on our back porch that we felt certain it had been our own black bear.

We never hunted again. Neither Dad nor I had the slightest yearning for the sport after that fateful Christmas. Oh, we still kept our tradition of walking out to old Weed Pond and trekking through the woods on our snowshoes and that was plenty fun for us. Occasionally, we could swear that we felt the eyes of an old black bear watching us through the clearing on the far side of the pond. We always backed away with respect.

This was her territory and, although we always felt that she was willing to share it, we had respect for her after that particular Christmas of Nineteen hundred and fifty- eight.

Something sacred and beautiful happened to us on that Christmas morning. Every year, as we sit around the fire, we laugh and remember. Oh, she still visits us now and then or perhaps her cub does, we are not sure. It is usually around Christmas Day that we hear the sound of crushed snow beneath huge paws, and the chomp of a nice dry leftover from an autumn pinecone.

And we know. . . .

We are Tsa la gi Cherokee

Granville Holt

Long, long ago we first offer thanksgiving
To the Season of red leaves and bare branches
When Deer coats are thick and Bear sleeps
And Earth Mother smiles as Spirit dawn
Teaches of her change in songs of promise

We circle the sacred fire to share blessings
And speak silent prayers to the four winds
Rising from ash to ember to flame as smoke
Drifts up to our Sun-Father's star nation
And we the Tsa la gi sing to seven humble ways

Secrets of days that keep us true to our tribe
We join with all man people in this dance
And remembrance of Creator-Spirit's love
Together we renew our life as Earth Mother
Turns her Seasons from planting to harvest to Winter

We are Tsa la gi

Spirits[2]

Janet K. Brennan

From Harriet Murphy, a Little Bit of Something

Right around a week before Thanksgiving, Minnie Wallace gave birth to a bouncing baby boy to whom she gave the proud name of Henry Wadsworth. I don't think you will have to go too far back in your own memory to remember that varmint of a man who was once the love of my own life. Being of sound mind and body and not knowing the history behind my sudden loathing for the other Henry Wadsworth, I could say nothing but nod in sweet affirmation of such a fine name. Each time she referred to her darling little baby, Henry W, I thought of that wonderful author and poet by the same name, and everything seemed to go down smooth as Irish whiskey on a cold winter night. She never did question me when I suddenly began to call the little one by the name of Hank, rather than Henry and, before I knew it, the whole town of Old Pine was referring to her new babe as Hank. Oddly enough, everyone but Smithy, who for some odd reason preferred his Christian name of Henry.

The almanac said we were going to have a long, cold winter, and so I had to take them as my bible for they did not ever steer me wrong. My apples that year were some of my proudest, and I began making my apple brown sugar pies for Thanksgiving early that year. I placed them in my cooler for safekeeping. Everyone would be coming to my own cabin that year and, by everyone I mean the Wallace Clan, Smithy the shoer, Seb from Old Seb's Tavern, Rose Tender and of course yours truly, who would be doin' most of the cookin'. Minnie was going to make her spice cake with oatmeal frosting, Smithy would provide her raisin plum stuffing and, of course, old Seb would be providing the sprits. He promised to also provide the turkey, which he said he intended to shoot and pluck himself; that remained to be seen.

I was not in a particularly festive or thankful mood that year. Much had happened that I was still in the process of questioning by way of heartache, death and lost love. It seemed to me that we could all use a bit of good luck in order to celebrate this day of thanks to the Lord.

The story I am about to tell you still rattles my bones, and yet telling it makes me somehow feel better. Not only did the happenstance of the occasion forever change my body, but it also changed my spirit in ways that I will never forget.

After the days of the rush for gold, many of the old mine shafts were simply left abandoned as they sank deep into the innards of the earth. Usually it was because there wasn't gold in the mine to begin with, but often it was because toward the end of the rush, bringing out the mineral was hardly worth the task, so most folks just hightailed it back to where they came from, empty handed with nothing to show except a few rattlesnake bites. The critters liked to hide in the cool wood casings and rock of the mines, usually about ten feet down from the surface of the shaft. In the state of California alone, by the turn of the century there were tens of thousands of old abandoned mines. As you might guess, there were problems from those holes in the ground as well as the tunnels that crisscrossed the ground underneath the hills of the Tahoe. Jennie Stillman lost her dog to one of the mines. The critter wandered off, fell into the mine and was stuck down there for eight weeks. They

---

[2] *Spirits* was previously published in "Harriet Murphy: A Little Bit of Something" by Janet K. Brennan, 2009, Casa de Snapdragon LLC

finally got him out, but he had starved to death in the wait for his owners to find him. It had not been a pretty sight, and Jenny suffered from nightmares for years. There was also a story goin' 'round about a cabin over in Placerville that sank into the ground. The hole just opened up and gobbled up everything in the house, residents and all. I was pretty dang sure that Daddy had built our cabin on solid ground as, being a miner himself, he pretty much knew where all of the mines in the area were located. All the same, every time my little daughter, Rose Tender, wandered too far from the porch, she would hear me call, "Don't go too far, Rosie, there are holes in the ground that can swallow up a little girl like you. Moreover, there are spirits in them mines. Spirits that don't like little girls." That always did it for her. I would barely get the sentence out when I would see her hair floppin' in the breeze as she hightailed it back to the porch.

Thanksgiving Day arrived bright and sunny in the morning, but as noon approached, the clouds were beginning to build in the northern sky. My best friend, Smithy, arrived early to help me set the table and tend to the last of the cooking of the turkey that Seb had shot only the day before.

"Ma'am Harriet, can we set an extra place for my mama?" asked Rose Tender.

We had so many holidays with Rose Tender and Chastity, it only seemed the proper thing to do.

"Yes, and I will go out with Pager, my horse, for a bit. He needs to run. I will also pluck the last of the fall marigolds up on the hill for our table."

"Don't be long," warned Smithy. "The weather is about to turn. The guests will be arriving shortly."

With those words from my friend, I set upon my way. There was indeed a brisk wind coming down the mountain, and I decided to make the trip as short as possible, allowing my quarter to run his legs a bit and gather the intended flowers for the table.

As we reached the top of the hill, Pager suddenly backed up on his hind legs. Spooked by a snake, he threw me over his right flank. Down I went, down and down and down. I was aware that I had passed through the ground and was falling into a hole big enough to swallow a house and a horse all at the same time. When I awoke, I found myself laying at the bottom of an old mine shaft with nary a sight of my quarter at the opening of the huge hole. My body hurt in all places that a body should not hurt, and I could not move my right leg.

"Help! Somebody help!" I called. "Pager! Pager! Where are you? Help."

Darkness enveloped me and when next I awoke, the sky was beginning to get black. Bits of icy rain fell and began choking the mouth of my prison. It splashed into the murky water that now filled the bottom of the mineshaft. I could see several dark tunnels leading off in different directions, but could not raise myself to investigate beyond a slight lean on my elbow. Several feet from me was a den, and two rattlers were curled around the opening not willing to look in my direction, which suited me just fine at that point in time. Although I was scrapped and bleeding, I soon discovered that I had not broken anything in the fall, which seemed like a miracle to me, as it had to have been at least a fifty-foot drop to the point in the shaft where my body had come to rest. I supposed bouncing off the walls on the way down had broken my fall.

"Help me, somebody help me. It is me, Harriet Dang Murphy. I am lost in this mine. I am cold and I need help getting out of this hell hole."

Was it my imagination? I thought I heard footsteps, possibly hoof steps, as Pager may have lingered not far from the mine. Bits of dirt fell from the opening. However, what in Sam Hell could the horse do? The last time I saw a four-legged critter jump into a mineshaft and rescue its captive was never. Sure as a sure-footed mule, which I could have used 'round about that time, Pager whinnied and then disappeared from the mine site.

I knew that my guests would be wondering where I was. Would they search? I was fairly sure that Pager would hightail it back to the cabin and, without me upon her backside, they would surely know that something had happened to me. But no one came, and the sky grew darker. The snow fell harder, until my body was covered in a thin layer of ice. Darkness descended such as nothing I had ever seen before, as the wind whistled through the trees far above my head.

"Harriet, Harriet," it called through whispers and sighs. "We are with you, Harriet."

Yes, and so were the rattlers, as I felt a sudden stinging in my leg when I tried to move it away from the den. I could see nothing, but instinctively knew that I had been bitten. It wasn't the first time a rattler bit me. It only takes one bite from such a demon to forever remember what it feels like. I had survived the last attack, and I would do the same with this one.

Crazy thoughts scurried through my head.

Oh, I hope Smithy minded that turkey and took her out when the time was right. Oh, I should have thought to set an extra place for Mother, I always did that. Did the folks remember that my apple brown sugar pies were resting in the cooler? Well, Rosie would tell them. She knew.

Of all years, this was the year to remember Thanksgiving Grace. I suddenly recalled all of the wonderful things to be thankful for. Until now, I had simply dwelled upon the misfortunes of the year. Forefront on my mind had been the sorrowful events that had transpired, barely giving a thought to the warmth of my home, the love of Rose Tender, and all of my friends. Smithy had come back into my life because I had invited her to do so, and she was happy for it. So was I. Lives had been lost and lives had been born almost immediately afterward… *the way of the world*, the way it should be - the plan of life. The crops had been fine, the lilac tree had come back to life, and the fire had stayed away from the cabin. As I drifted off to sleep again, a dream entered through my mind quick as a lightning bolt on a hot summer night. Old Seb raised his glass in salute to everyone sitting in his friendly establishment. "*Here's to good times, good wines, and may your spirit be as strong as the one that fills this cup.*" Next, it was Cousin Claire's bangle. It was the very one that she had left to me, the one that lost the center jade stone when I fell in the storm and dang near drowned in the river. There were crazy thoughts, crazy dreams. Rose Tender was calling me, through the snow. She was crying, and each time that I reached for her, she disappeared. A dog's emaciated and hollow eyes stared deeply into mine, pleading, save me.

At long last, morning light drifted through the opening of the mine. It was hard to tell how long I had been sleeping, but a good guess told me it had been at least twelve hours or so. Yet, no one had come. Dang, I didn't know this mine was here and I had lived here all of my life. They surely would not know.

Raising my body, bruised, bleeding and snake bitten, I managed to stand and survey the side of the mine. The wood lining the sides would not hold my weight. It was rotten and filled with varmint holes and mold. I tried and fell back down upon my swollen and aching foot.

"Help me! help me! It is Harriet and I am struck down here forever if someone does not come along." I could not stand the thought that I would spend another day and night in this prison, and tears of frustration and fear came upon me. "Not now, Lord. Not like this, please!"

Suddenly I heard a sound. A rope, long and thick, fell from the opening of the mine. It swung just above my head and I grabbed it. Someone had come to find me, although I heard not a sound. Grabbing the rope, I held it tightly with my freezing hands. They were numb and it took every ounce of concentration not to let go. Soon, I felt myself being hoisted from the bottom of the shaft as the light at the top grew larger and larger, and I could finally feel cool air against my face. When the tugging stopped, I used what I could of my feet to climb my way to the top and managed to crawl a distance from the hole. The snow was thick around me, and I could just barely make out the figure of a human walking off toward the cabin. I could not tell if it was a man or a woman, the snow was too thick.

My God, they don't know it is me. They don't realize that they have rescued me. "Hey, come back. It is me, Harriet. You saved me, git me home!"

In a half walk and crawl I forged my way through the snow and down the mountain toward the cabin. Old Seb was standing on the back porch. I could barely see his figure as he was enveloped in smoke from the stogie that he was puffing away on. He saw me.

"Harriet, Harriet. My God, it is Harriet."

Arms came around me and lifted me into my home. Pulling my clothes off and placing me into my bed, they covered me with thick blankets from my closet. I fell off to sleep and when I awoke the doc was there putting ice on my legs, foot and wounds. He then offered me a good cup of the Irish, which warmed my insides in a delicious and comfortable way. I giggled. He then proceeded to cut the venom from my leg.

"Frost bite," I heard him say. "Snake bite. But a miracle that she is still with us, though she is going to lose her foot. I don't know how I will tell her." I heard him, but did not comprehend.

Rose Tender approached me with a smile. "Harriet, Ma'am. Did an old hole come and swallow you? Were there evil spirits? We have put all of the food away until you are better and then we will have our Thanksgiving Dinner."

"Who pulled you from the mine?" asked Smithy, tearful and anxious. "We will invite him to our Thanksgiving Dinner. Where is he?"

"My dear, I have no idea who pulled me from the hole. I watched as he disappeared into the snow and called after him, but he did not hear me nor turn. It could have been a woman for all I know, although I doubt that a woman would have that kind of strength. Whoever it was, barely gave me a thought after pulling me from the mine."

"Well, don't give it a thought. We will find the man, and he will join us when you are ready"

Two days passed with tender loving care from all, and this would be the day we were to celebrate our Thanksgiving Dinner. No one had come forth to claim the rescue and, as I dressed carefully in a new dress that Minnie had purchased for me the day before from Sears and Roebuck, I gathered my wet clothes from the floor. They were still wet.

"Best burn these, Minnie. I do not care to recall that experience in this life time." Suddenly, out of the rear pocket fell a stone, brilliant green in color and shiny as new.

"Why, it is a jade stone," cried Minnie. "What in the world?"

"Minnie, that is the stone that fell from Cousin Claire's bauble the night I almost lost the gift in the storm. Could it have been inside of my pocket all of this time?"

That day, as we gathered around our Thanksgiving Table, we had much to be thankful for. The turkey and stuffing were cooked to perfection, my apple brown sugar pies warmed on the oven, and the aroma of fresh spice filled the cabin. Rose Tender had set a place at the table for her mother and next to it, I placed two more; one for my own mother and one for the spirit who had saved my life. Seb raised his glass high in the air

"Here's to good times, fine wines, and may your spirit be as strong as the one that fills this cup."

Everyone nodded in solemn and happy approval as I pulled a fine, green stone from the pocket of my new dress and placed it on one of the empty plates at the table. "I think we can all agree, Seb. The spirits are fine my friend. The spirits are just fine!

Misty Morn on Old Gray Pond

Janet K. Brennan

Winter fire burns
stoked with pinion cones
welcoming me to this day.
Remembering, quick prayers sighed
before falling to dreams.
A promise whispered through the night
that with the sun-rising
a world finds peace.

.

As light peeps through window-frost,
I cannot sleep
for the gathering birds,
as choirs of seraphim singing
on Old Gray Pond.

.

Stepping into the misty morn,
still- water reflects mountains,
painted white,
leaning close, inhaling
peace of God's lake shrine.

.

Loons, distant call through reeds,
announce praise
for lion, lamb to embrace.
Sustenance divine, this place
to soothe souls wounded
in battles lost - a world undone.

.

Holy day on old Gray Pond.
For all to bathe in healing mists
revel in the knowledge;
peace begets peace and we are one,
a new beginning.

.

Is this a dream,
or am I first to take a place
along the misty shore?

.

If I reach and touch another,
and they the same, I will know.

.

My hands entwined with other hands,
warm embraces filled with love
whisper in the wind of truth.

.

This is the day the world begins,
this misty morn on old Gray Pond.

Margaret's Painted Horse

Janet K. Brennan

This is a Christmas story. I cannot call it anything other than that, but you may beg to differ. It happened during one of the Christmases that Grace O'Donnell and her husband, Matthew, and daughter, Margaret, experienced a happenstance quite odd in the small village of Deer's Ridge, New Hampshire. I will relay this story as clearly as I remember it, and I remember it well, for I was there.

Grace O'Donnell had recently lost a baby in the autumn before that Yule Tide and had fallen into the darkest depression of her life. Although Christmas was fast approaching, she could not bring herself to shop or wrap gifts. Simply leaving the house was extremely difficult. And so, she limited her trips to her neighbors, or quick walks down the paths that surrounded her farm.

Now let me tell you, Deer's Ridge, a beautiful, rural New England village is nestled in the hills just north of Concord. One might expect to see it on the front of a Hallmark Greeting Card with its tiny Main Street, quaint little shops, and a small church with a picket fence surrounding the cemetery just across the street. For the most part, Deer's Ridge was a farming community where the same families had lived for generations, passing their acreages down from child to child. At Christmas time it was especially beautiful with each home lit with white candles. They burned in the shuttered windows for all to see.

During the Christmas that I am writing about, the weather was abominable. The Farmer's Almanac had predicted a particularly nasty and snowy winter, and it had proven to be accurate. A week before Christmas, it began to snow and except for a few spits of icy rain and pearl gray skies, it seldom let up.

"Mum, c'mon," begged Margaret. "Let's go into town and buy some Christmas presents. Please, please!"

Although Grace dreaded it, off they went down the five mile road that led to the small village of Deer's Ridge "I want to get back before it gets dark, Margaret. I don't want to be on the road in this weather any longer than necessary," said Grace.

This day would be Grace's first outing since the death of her babe, and the closer they got to town, the faster her heartbeat. In the center of the village is a great, old time restaurant by the name of The Rusty Scupper and, though they specialized in the best chowder north of Boston, both Grace and her daughter, Margaret, enjoyed huge plates stacked with griddlecakes smothered in fresh maple syrup. Then they walked up Main Street. They wandered in and out of the shops, purchasing gifts for Matthew, as well as trinkets for each other to put under the tree on Christmas morning. I might add that Grace O'Donnell was known for her sweet mince pies, which she generously baked for all of her neighbors for their Christmas Table. Therefore, a stop at the market was necessary for some last minute spices and raisins. Just as they were ready to turn back to their four-wheel, they passed a small shop. In the window was a beautiful, brown, painted horse.

"Oh, mum, look! Isn't it gorgeous! Now, that is what I want for Christmas."

"Margaret, dear . . . that is for a small child. See, it has rockers on the bottom. Now what would you do with such a thing?"

"Why, I would keep it in my room and then someday when I have children, say in about ten years, it would belong to them."

Grace could feel the laughter bubbling from somewhere deep inside of her, and it was a sound that she had not heard for a very long time. "You had better make that twenty years, little girl. I will not be ready to be a grandmother in ten years, And you, sweetie, will not be ready to be a mother!"

"Can we go in, please, just to look at it? Not to buy, just to touch it. See how beautiful that mane of yarn is, and those black button eyes look so real."

Before she knew it, Grace was following Margaret into the store. Margaret shook the little jingle bell that hung around its neck.

"She's lovely, aint she, Gracie?" came the deep vibrato of Tim Walton from behind his counter. "She was dropped off by a little indigent girl. I'm selling her on consignment. Poor thing carved the horse herself. Needs money pretty bad, being with child and all. She can't be more than sixteen years old. I have not seen her around for several days. For a while, she came in to see if the horse had sold, but lately, I have not seen her."

"Well, we are not interested. Tim, Margaret admires the horse, but is just a bit too old for it. I was thinking along the lines of faded jeans and perhaps a few Pink Floyd recordings."

Margaret rolled her eyes.

"Too bad, Grace, I may have to put her up in storage until next year if that girl doesn't come back to claim her."

That night, Grace O'Donnell patted herself on her back for having successfully maneuvered a day in town with very few problems and resolved to do it far more often. She busied herself with baking mince pies to take to Sam Johnson who lived on a lovely working farm. He always hinted 'round about Thanksgiving time that he hoped she would be doing her usual fine baking of pies at Christmas.

After sinking into a hot tub and inhaling the wet, warm steam, there was a gentle rap on the bathroom door.

"Mum, did you know that there is a loose horse in our yard?"

"A loose horse, are you certain?"

"Yes, it was right outside my bedroom window. I am afraid it may be lost. The snow is coming down very hard."

"Well, there is little that we can do about it tonight, but tomorrow, when I take the pies up to the Johnson farm, I will see if he is missing one of his geldings."

Coincidentally, that was the same night that Grace was able to go into the prepared baby nursery that now lay empty. It was also the first night that she did not fall to her knees in tears.

The following day, a determined Grace O'Donnell trudged through the snow up to the Johnson farm. Johnson assured her that all of his horses were in the barn for the winter and that none had gone missing. "Perhaps you were dreaming, Margaret. You know how carried away you have been about that painted horse at Tim Walton's toy store," said Grace.

~~

The week leading up to Christmas was a busy one. Grace baked and prepared sumptuous goodies for their Christmas Dinner. Before they knew it, Christmas Eve arrived. Although every Christmas Eve seemed a special, holy night, this particular Christmas Eve seemed even more sacred. The falling of the snow had made everything appear as a winter wonderland, and a hush fell over the village of Deer's Ridge. Even the church bells calling everyone to service seemed to ring in a blessed, hushed reverence.

Just as Matt O'Donnell was preparing to hop into bed, they suddenly heard the banging of the barn door in the wind.

"Dang, Matt . . . I will go and secure it, I am still dressed. Donning her heaviest wool coat, boots and warm fur hat that Margaret had given her the Christmas prior, she carefully made her way down the path to the barn. Stopping in her tracks, she thought that she saw the figure of a horse standing just outside the barn doors. Then it was gone. Locking the doors up tight and heading back to the house, she saw it again. This time it was approaching her, neighing and eager to greet.

"Mum, Mum!" shouted Margaret running from the house. "It is her, see? I told you. She belongs to someone. Her name is Daisy. It is on the tag just below her neck."

"Well, we have no room for her here. I will ride her up to Johnson's Farm and see if he has an open stall. You go back inside. I will be back shortly," said Grace.

Mounting the horse, Grace gave her a quick kick and off they went. However, it would seem that the horse had other ideas about just where they would go. Faster than a shooting star on Christmas night, Grace was carried off in the opposite direction. They flew down the road that headed toward town, and then veered off across a snow-covered meadow to an old abandoned stable. Stopping just outside its doors, she dismounted and could see the slight flicker of a lantern inside. Soon the scream of a girl in horrible pain filled the night air. Entering the stable, Grace saw a young girl in the far corner. She was giving birth, and she was alone.

"Help me, Ma'am. Please, my baby is coming. I fear I am going to die. The pain is so great. Please help me." A quick look at the young girl's situation immediately told Grace that a baby was about to come into the world. "Yes, honey. Your baby's head is crowning. Give some good strong pushes and we will get it out . . . push, push!"

No sooner had she said the words than out came the most beautiful little baby girl she had ever seen. With a holler, a prayer, and a quick cleansing of its face, she laid the baby girl across her mother's breasts. Quickly covering her with her coat, she piled what little bit of dry hay that she could find around them both.

"I am going for help. Lay still and you both will be just fine."

Hightailing it back up the road on Daisy's back, they found Farmer Johnson locking up his barn for the night. "We'll get her to the clinic in town. Not many folks working on Christmas Eve. It will be a skeleton crew, but if we can get them there, they should be fine."

That night, after making sure mother and child were safe and warm within the walls of the tiny clinic on Main Street, Grace wandered back up to where her truck was parked. There it was! Tim Walton had not sold the painted horse, and he was just closing up for the night.

"Wait, Tim . . . wait! I am going to buy that horse for Margaret after all. If you will just give me a hand loading her into the back of the truck, I will not bother you again. I have a feeling that little girl who carved it will be coming by to claim her money very soon."

~~~

Margaret was thrilled to find her painted horse under the tree the following morning and, as she examined her every detail, she cried.

"Oh look, Mum! See the tag around its neck, her name is Daisy!"

"Well, how very strange!" declared Grace, with no small amount of wonder. "It seems as if there are just some very odd happpenstances that just defy explanation."

The O'Donnell family spent Christmas day at the little clinic. Grace stopped by her own nursery at home and pulled one of the untouched stuffed bears from a small shelf and placed it in her basket of goodies, which contained some other small gifts and a mine pie. She loved knowing that a baby would play with that bear after all.
~~~

"My name is Jessie, and I cannot thank you enough, Ma'am. I have no family in these parts. I came to work at the five and dime and lost my job when things got tough. If it had not been for you, I may have died in that old stable." She had seen no horse that night or any other night. Neither had any of the humble people living in Deer's Ridge. It would seem that only Grace and Margaret had seen Daisy. Moreover, they would never see her again. It was just one of those unexplainable happenstances.

<div align="center">~~~</div>

Well, my babe and I lived and loved with the wonderful O'Donnell family until I was strong enough to leave and work at my old job at the five and dime. We became a part of the family, and that empty nursery that Grace had so lovingly prepared for her own baby did not stay empty for very long. Moreover, although none of us ever saw Daisy again, the story still goes 'round and 'round that somewhere in those beautiful, snow covered meadows just north of Concord, where the wind whispers gentle secrets through the pine trees, there lives a beautiful horse by the name of Daisy. She belongs to no one and everyone all at the same time. And, even if we should forget one year to light a Christmas Candle in honor of her, we could never forget her, for we will always have Margaret's painted horse to remind us.

A Christmas Prayer

Janet K. Brennan

As silver strands
soften the pre-dawn sky
melt to lovely shades of amber,
Snowy Owl, feathers plump,
nestles quietly, eyes fixed
heralding a rising sun.
May we pray , thankful
for His glorious gift
of another most holy
celebration.

May peace and joy be with you,

Jan and Art

The Twelve Days of Christmas[3]

Janet K. Brennan

It was Christmas. The snow that gently hugged the tips of the mountains and the farolitos that graced the homes and business establishments in the desert southwest, told me so. It was not Christmas in my heart. My children were busy with their holiday parties and simply doing the perfunctory baking of cookies for them was a massive chore. You see, tragedy struck our family just four months earlier by way of the untimely and sad death of my oldest daughter, Kristen.

Much to my surprise, life proceeded, albeit on a surreal level. How would I get through the holidays? How could I be strong for my family?

Christmas was just two weeks away and my parents decided to fly out and join us. They had not weathered the death of their Grandchild well. It was good that we would all be together for this holiday. Little did we know what was about to happen to us that Christmas.

It was a quiet night. The lights of Albuquerque sparkled below us and I had just finished playing Christmas songs on my piano, when the front door bell chimed. My son, Nick, was quick to see who had come to visit us this late.

"What in the world?" He exclaimed. "There's no one here."

My daughter, Kate, ran to the door and gasped in surprise. Sitting on the front porch was a beautiful, white candle covered in a glass dome. The fire of the candle danced merrily, and we quickly brought it inside. How nice! Who could have given us such a nice present? Why didn't they stay so that we could thank them? So many questions!

The following night, after a particularly stressful day, we once again heard the sound of the doorbell. The children laughed merrily. This time, a basket of freshly baked ginger cookies was left for us. They were still warm and were covered with a clean red-checkered, dishtowel. Nick quickly ran out onto the porch and into the driveway. No one was there.

What was going on? Who could be doing this? How could they disappear into the night so quickly without a trace?

On the third night, we waited with anticipation. Nick had a plan that he felt would be foolproof. He would be ready this time, should the doorbell ring. He camped out in the foyer, directly in front of the door. Sure enough, this time, there came a knock. Before anyone had a chance to respond, Nick swung open the door. However, much to his chagrin, he had not been fast enough. Nestled amongst delicate, green foil, were two crystal tree ornaments. They were filled with a fragrant, spicy potpourri. We immediately placed them in a prominent location on our Christmas tree. This was fun! My father's eyes sparkled with life, and my mother's face was lit with a happy smile. How wonderful! Someone was playing the "Twelve Days of Christmas" on us. Who could be doing such a wonderful thing?

The fourth night arrived, accompanied by a storm. Wind and snow lapped against our windows with a fury, and we were certain that we would not receive a visit from our Christmas Ghost on such a dreary and cold night. We were wrong! Right on schedule, the front door rattled with a knock, and this time, two tiny wooden angels with starched, lace wings were left behind for us to behold. The children ran to the end of the porch. Nothing could be seen, not even a footprint in the

---

[3] The Twelve Days of Christmas was previously published in Chicken Soup for the Soul Christmas, 2008

snow. Such a mystery!

On the fifth, sixth and seventh nights, we received tall, honey wax candles, a nut bread bursting with cherries and almonds, and a tiny nut cracker carved from clothes pins and held together with pipe cleaners, Now it was time to get down to serious business. Our curiosity was piqued. We simply had to know who our mystery benefactor was.

"No," said my father. "Whoever it is, does not want to be seen, and it is our responsibility to keep it that way. This is part of the gift. This Angel is also receiving a gift, the pure and obvious joy of giving, secure in the knowledge that he or she is bringing joy into this family at a very difficult time."

He, of course, was right.

On the eighth night, we waited. No one came. Disappointed and tired, we went to bed. We had come to look forward to our nocturnal visits, and wondered why they had stopped. Morning dawned brightly and, when my husband stepped outside to retrieve his paper, lo and behold! On our threshold were two gifts . . . a red poinsettia and a lovely Christmas cactus which was preparing to bloom. Our friend had truly caught us off guard this time. Indeed, our eighth and ninth day gifts had been quietly left outside of our door sometime during the night.

On the tenth night, we received an apple pie, steaming hot and carefully wrapped in red and green napkins. On the twelfth day, brown and white, handmade coasters made of cardboard and lined with satin ribbon were left. So lovely!

Christmas Eve was upon us, and it had happened so quickly, that we forgot to be sad. Our sweet Angel had taken our minds off our loss and had treated us to a very different kind of Christmas. It was one that we had never anticipated. Each night, the children had run outside in a vain effort to catch a glimpse of our benevolent friends, and yet, on the twelfth night, we still had no idea who had so diligently and kindly bestowed us with its sweet blessings.

On the twelfth day, Christmas Day, we sat in the living room. All of our gifts had been exchanged, and we had enjoyed a quiet, family dinner. It had been a good Christmas after all, loving and joyous. Then, as usual, the front door bell rang. Right on cue, our secret Santa disappeared into the night, leaving behind a small, white envelope. Upon opening it, we found that our twelfth Christmas gift was a message, neatly written in a child's hand.

It read:

I am the spirit of Christmas
That is PEACE
I am the spirit of gladness . . . HOPE
I am the heart of Christmas that is LOVE
Have a Merry Christmas!

We were changed from that night on. We began to heal. Going on with our lives seemed a bit easier. We never knew who left all of those wonderful gifts. We did divine the "Spirit of Christmas" and how important it is to take the time to be friends. We learned how essential it is to bring a bit of sunshine into a dark place . . . not simply at Christmas, but all year through.

Joanna and the Magi

Florence B. Weinberg

A Christmas Story

Afterward he journeyed from one town and village to another, preaching and proclaiming the good news of the kingdom of God. Accompanying him were the Twelve and some women who had been cured of evil spirits and infirmities, Mary, called Magdalene, from whom seven demons had gone out, Joanna, the wife of Herod's steward Chuza, Susanna, and many others who provided for them out of their resources.
— Luke 8:1-3

The women sat on a rise above the Sea of Galilee, as Jesus blessed the crowd, ending his lesson. He began healing the many sick ones lying before him today, something that could take at least an hour, and the women knew they had time to exchange stories of their experiences. Five women had stories to tell, so they drew straws and Joanna's was the shortest. The others clustered close around her to listen.

I was eleven then. My father Eliab was Herod's steward before my husband Chuza, and I had the run of the palace, though I was quiet about it. It is wise to be quiet in Herod's palace. The king, his family, the courtiers and the servants were used to seeing me and paid little attention to my comings and goings.

One day, as I watched the streets from my lofty perch on the roof of the palace, I saw a camel train winding its way toward the palace front gate. At its head were three brilliant figures — they looked like kings — in silks with golden trim and gold chains around their necks. One wore yellow; he was in his middle years with curly, black hair and a square beard. One wore red, a stately elderly man with a long white beard. One wore green. He had ebony black skin with no beard. I had seen a few visitors like him before, but none so imposing.

The camels knelt, the impressive men dismounted, and the guards admitted them into the palace courtyard along with four servants carrying what looked like gifts. The rest stayed outside. I ran downstairs in my bare feet to watch what they did then.

By the time I arrived, they had presented their gifts to King Herod. I peeked around the doorframe. The black-beard spoke for all three and asked permission to follow the star deeper into Herod's realm.

"What star? Why? What do you seek?" the king asked.

"We seek a child who is the newborn king of the Jews. We saw his star at its rising and have come to do him homage."

The king's brows drew together in a black line. He looked deeply troubled. "A new king? I must consider your request."

He dismissed them until the following day. "Come to me tomorrow at this time," he told them, "and I will tell you if you may seek farther for this newborn king." He then summoned his servants, including my father Eliab, and ordered them to make the potentates that he called magi comfortable for a day.

A great stir arose in the palace. The king sent messengers throughout Jerusalem to gather the priests and the scribes, the Pharisees and the Sadducees, for consultation. They remained in session with him for hours. My father, who personally supervised refreshments for them, overheard their conclusion: the new king was the Messiah, who was to be born in Bethlehem of Judea, the city of David, for the prophet had written:

> And you, Bethlehem of Judah, are by no
>   means least among the rulers of Judah;
> since from you shall come a ruler,
>   who is to shepherd my people Israel.

The next day at the appointed time, the three magi again met with King Herod.

"When did this star appear?" he demanded.

"It rose four months ago, Your Majesty," the white-bearded magus in red silk told him.

"My wise men have told me the child is to be found in Bethlehem," the king said. "Go and search throughout that city for him and when you have found him, bring me word, that I, too, may go and do him homage."

He dismissed them then, and after they had passed through the door, he called his wife Herodias to him.

She said, "My Lord, you are troubled. What is it? What evil tidings did the strangers bring?"

"They told me that a new king of the Jews was born, that they have seen his star at its rising and have come to do him homage. My priests and scribes have said he is to be found in Bethlehem. The magi will return to me after they have worshipped him and will tell me where to find him. I fear this child. What am I to do?"

"Do what your heart tells you, My Lord. But surely, you would not allow a viper to flourish and grow in your pleasure garden."

"Wife, you indeed divine the secrets of my heart. When I learn the nesting-place of this young viper, I will crush his head under my heel."

I had been hiding among the dusty, deep read draperies behind the throne and that fell in heavy pleats on each side. I heard every word. I must warn the magi! The strangers would wait until dusk before leaving, since they were still following the star. As soon as it was safe, I hurried to my cousin Abidan's rooms. He is my age and about my size.

"Abidan, I need to leave the palace tonight. May I borrow some of your clothes? You know a girl can't be seen alone on the streets, especially after dark, but I could pass easily for a boy."

"Why would you need to go out after dark?"

"I can't tell you now but I promise to tell you the whole story later."

Abidan's face showed his doubt and reluctance. "I don't know…"

"Please, Abidan, what harm could it do to lend me your tunic, a belt, your head-covering and your sandals? I'll bring them all back tomorrow."

"Maybe. That's not much to ask, but you're always up to some mischief, Joanna, and you'd better not get me in trouble over this!"

"No mischief this time, Abidan, I promise!"

"Hmmm." He hesitated, then at last, "All right then, if you bring the things back tomorrow." He rummaged in a chest and brought out a clean but worn tunic, a belt, a head-wrap and some ancient sandals.

"Here; I suppose these will do?"

"Oh, thank you, Abidan! You're a real friend!"

I wanted to hug him, but knew he would only push me away. I took the clothes and ran back to my room. I waited until the sun was about to set. "Mother," I said, "you remember I was invited to Leah's house for supper and to stay the night. I've decided to go out after all. I know you trust her mother Rebecca, so you know I'll be safe. I promise to be good. So may I go? Please?"

I felt guilty, because, although I'd not actually lied, I had badly bent the truth. I kept my fingers crossed behind my back the whole time and prayed that God would forgive me for misleading my dearest mother. She thought for only a moment.

"Yes, you may go, since the house is right next door. But don't go out until there's no one in the street, and keep your face covered until you're inside their house. Also, keep your promise to be good—you and Leah both!"

"I will, Mama dear!" I gave her a big hug and ran off to dress as a boy. It was easy to hide my hair under the head-wrap, and the tunic, belt, and ancient sandals fitted very well. I tiptoed out of my room and crept down the stairs so Mama wouldn't see how I was dressed.

The caravan, just outside the palace gates, was clustered around the gate, the camels—great smelly beats that looked foul-tempered—crouched on their bellies in their finery. Only the magi were missing. Then the three came out, and a servant bowed and helped each one mount his camel. The beasts rose with much guttural grumbling.

"Look!" The ebony-skinned man in the green silk robes pointed east. "The star is rising! It's moving! It will guide us to the child."

And they set out. I mingled with the servants who accompanied the caravan on foot. They paid no attention to me, since their eyes were fixed on the star—as were mine. Before we left the city, I stepped on half of a broken water jar in the dark. It flipped with a clatter, and the sharp broken edge barely missed my sandaled foot. I pushed it to the side of the street and walked on, thanking God for saving my foot as well as my purpose.

The night seemed magical. The heavens were a deep purple, hung with skeins of tiny, twinkling stars that were dwarfed by the blazing yellow star we followed. The night air, once we were outside the city, wafted perfume from blossoms somewhere out there in the darkness. We walked for a long time along the dusty road. The camel beside me swept his head around to lick an itchy spot on his side; his bit caught in my head-cover and pulled it off. My long hair tumbled down, suddenly exposing me as a girl! I pulled the head-cover loose as the beast swung his head back and quickly placed it on my head, tucking my hair inside. Would I be expelled from the group? Oddly, no one had noticed—their eyes were either still trained on the star above or on their feet as they avoided rocks and holes in the road. God had kept me safe once again.

We came to the outskirts of a village where low houses of mud and stone, whitish in the starlight, showed flickering candlelight through their windows. I supposed it was Bethlehem. We moved through narrow, winding streets deeper into the town until the star seemed to stop over one of the houses. The lead magus, the man with the black beard, held up his hand and the caravan halted. The three camels knelt with many a groan, and the magi dismounted. The white-bearded one knocked on the door. After a moment, a nice-looking man about my father's age with brown hair and beard opened.

"Yes?"

"We are three astrologers from Persia, and have seen the star rising in the east, the one announcing the birth of the king of the Jews. We have come to worship him."

The nice-looking man hesitated only a moment while he gazed in amazement at the caravan, the camels in their fancy trappings, and especially at the three magi.

"Come in and welcome!" he said at last, "Others have come to do our son homage, but up to now none so distinguished." He turned toward the interior. "Mary my love, three kings have come to worship."

By this time, I had found a viewing place before a window, the servants grouped around me. We saw a beautiful young woman seated by a fireplace. Her glossy, long brown hair was draped with a blue scarf and she was holding a child in her lap, supporting him with one arm across his middle. A glow surrounded them both as if many candles were alight behind them. Was it just the firelight? I felt something like power streaming from the baby boy and knew that the prophets were right. Here was the infant Messiah! He sat straight up on his mother's knee with his little arms propped on hers. His eyes were focused on the doorway as if he knew what was happening.

All this I felt and saw in an instant, while Mary replied: "By all means, Joseph, let them come in!"

He bowed to the magi and opened the door wide. And in they came introducing themselves: Melchior, the eldest, first. He knelt and with a pretty speech presented a casket of gold coins. He held it close so the baby could see it. The child raised a hand as if in blessing. The second king, Gaspar of the black beard, presented a box that exhaled the most delightful scent. Frankincense, I thought. The baby lifted his head a little, inhaled and gurgled with delight. The third king, Balthazar, had brought myrrh. At this, the baby seemed to nod, as though acknowledging its great worth.

The kings—the magi—chanted prayers, thanked Mary and Joseph, and spoke with them informally for a while, then withdrew. Joseph showed them where a comfortable inn could house them all for the night. They mounted to move on to the inn, but I stayed behind to speak to Joseph, who lingered by the door to watch the magi's departure.

"Joseph, my father is Eliab, the steward in King Herod's palace. This is what I overheard. When the magi had left after telling him of the birth of the King of the Jews, the king consulted his wife. She said, 'Do what your heart tells you, My Lord, but surely you would not allow a viper to flourish and grow in your pleasure garden.' The king then vowed to destroy the 'viper,' as he called the new-born king, your son."

Joseph's face grew stiff and pale. "God help us! What should we do?"

I spoke as one inspired. "You must take Mary and the child and flee, sir. Herod expects the magi to return and tell him where you are. He will surely send his servants to slay you all."

"My child, you are a true messenger; an angel of God. I feel you speak for Him. We will do as you suggest."

"I thank the God of Israel that you believe me." Then, it struck me all at once in what danger I had placed myself and my whole family—and maybe Abidan and his family too. "But please, don't let anyone know how you were warned. It could get me, my family and friends killed. Please say an angel came to you in a dream."

"I understand and will say exactly that. An angel *did* come to me in a dream once…."

"Now, I must warn the magi, too."

"Go with God, my child."

I ran to catch up with the caravan and arrived just as the magi dismounted. "Sirs," I said, a bit breathless, "Please! Heed what I say. I am the child of Eliab the steward in Herod's palace, and I overheard what the king plans to do." I again repeated the words Herod and his wife had exchanged. "Please, you must not go back to Jerusalem or they will come and kill the newborn king."

The magi exchanged looks with raised eyebrows and nods. Gaspar said, "I told you that man acted strangely and was not to be trusted." He turned to me, leaning down with a grave look as though he took me quite seriously. "So, what is your advice, young master?"

"Return to your country by another way, My Lords. The road to Persia leads out of Bethlehem in the opposite direction from the road you entered by." I pointed.

Balthazar spoke up. "What word, then, should we leave behind?"

"Why not tell the innkeeper and the servants that a powerful dream warned you not to return to Herod. They will surely repeat that to Herod's people when they come. Yes, tell them it came to you in a dream."

Joanna paused, smiling at the other women with their rapt faces. "And so it is written that an angel of the Lord told Joseph in a dream to take Mary and the baby Jesus and flee — and he chose Egypt. It is also written that a dream informed the magi to return home by another way."

Mary Magdalene smiled as she glanced at Jesus, below on the seashore, healing the sick. "Now we know what really happened that night when the three magi came to worship. Joseph was right. You truly *were* God's angel."

Christmas Eve

Robert Mirabal

Lost in the direction of time and memory.
I have been here before but all seems so gray and wondrous.
Pitch pinewood consumed in fire at a safe conceivable distance to the east.
Dreams frenzied by forgetfulness.
Telling time by the Sun can be deceiving walking on the road to the pueblo Telling time by the Sun can be deceiving walking on the road to the pueblo.

Icy cold wind and my steps get me there slowly.
So far but so near, inside me is the past event.
I have become numb and bizarre.
But my glory is to keep my vision.
The world is not a place to be defined, especially in the winter, The world is not a place to be defined, especially in the winter.
The cold gives you a name.
"You are old, You are old, You are old, "
"I have become old."
The old pueblo walls greet my great return.
But they have kept their youthful brown faces.
Virgin Mary is floating on the trance of the minds of hundreds and thousands on Christmas eve, Virgin Mary is floating on the trance of the minds of hundreds and thousands on Christmas eve.
Suspended on a sea of swelling smoke, sailing through the environment of fire.
Sparkles of light and silver,
Across, across, they travel across the melted floor of the pueblo pushed by the environment of heat and cold, showing no way out.
Her silent prayers are for the ends of feuds of the world, Her silent prayers are for the ends of feuds of the world.
For her lost children dying on the seas---dying--on the seas.
I see you in a pose of prayer forever, you are silhouetted by the fury of bonfires and smoke.
Owls cry, so do coyotes and I cry to because we are alive, as you verge back down on the ancient racetrack.
There is no way out except to follow yourself back into your church.
It is your place of worship, standing, shivering as sinners enter.
Bon-fires assembly your way, gunfire's shot into the intention of darkness.
Feels like the war is over and just beginning.
Love is over, dropped on the ground for all to step on.
Hate is alive in the night but that too is sleepy, Hate is alive in the night but that too is sleepy on Christmas eve.
Return Mary sit, Return Mary sit. Mary sits,
Looking back at us waiting for the day when they no longer change your cloths.

Waiting for the day when it all falls apart.
Pine wood consumed in fire.
Smoke travels again up into the night sky.
It's Christmas Eve on the Taos pueblo.
It's windy among the icy cold.
The road to the village is so far, The road to the village is so far, But it still so near.
The cold gives you a name you are old, you are old..

At Winter Solstice[4]

Charles Adès Fishman

Everything is still today: filmed
with a pale blue grayness
The birches that glowed white
in late autumn sunlight have been
extinguished This is the cusp
of change

Midnight will open the brightest
blossom of moon but only if the gray veil
lifts only if we remain awake Now
is the time to bring in the ancient tree —
quick, while its green fires cast
such a sober light

Hold back from adornment:
it will grow darker yet before this night swells
and turns toward bleak cold morning
before desire stirs each slumbering root
and the first bright sparks of color appear
Go deeper still into waiting:

be like the mist and shadow and praise
the oncoming night that races
toward its final wingbeat of darkness.

---

[4] *At Winter Solstice* was previously published in "Country of Memory" by Charles Adès Fishman, 2011, Uccelli Press

The Holiday Ride

Janet K. Brennan

Germany was everything I had hoped it would be! It was filled with mystical castles on far away hills, little streams that ran though tiny, quaint villages that always seemed to smell of rich fires burning in old chimneys. I could not wait to get out and investigate this lush and green country, which would be our new home for the next three years.

Landing in Frankfurt on a sweet, autumn day, Kristen, my oldest daughter, and Kate, just three, could not wait to be reunited with Art, my husband. We had been apart for three long months, and now we could be a family again.

Our home would be in temporary quarters just outside the tiny village of Münchweiler in the Rhineland-Palatinate district of Germany, several kilometers from Pirmasens on the French border. It was a large apartment on the top floor.

Three months later, I felt the familiar symptoms of pregnancy. That did not stop us as a family, and we managed to travel around this beautiful and very ancient country with its villages often surrounded in mist and rivers that seemed to melt into the hills they were forged from. Springtime brought beautiful window boxes with hanging geraniums, and edelweiss sprung from the meadows, which surrounded our village. It also brought permanent living quarters in Pirmasens, and we were thrilled. This was a luxury for us. Now Kristen could go to the American school on the base, and we could walk to the commissary and PX. This was a good thing since most of the time our little German Taunus did not run.

By the end of the summer, I was large and had a difficult time getting up off the sofa without the help of Art. This was baby number three, due sometime in December.

During my last three months of pregnancy, I had to travel to the hospital in Landstuhl for my appointments. Landstuhl was a lovely, little city that boasted its own castle just a stone's throw from the hospital. It was almost a two-hour drive, and I began to think about the possibility of having my baby at home for fear of not being able to make it to the hospital on time. I knew from my previous deliveries that when I went into labor, I came fast and furious, and the drive between Pirmasens and Landstuhl was a lonely stretch of back roads through the mountains.

The months passed quickly, and before we knew it, Christmas was upon us. Christmas time in Germany is a festive and joyful time. All of the cities and villages set up their Christmas Fairs called Krismart. Throughout the country, Christmas markets—sometimes known as Kris Kringle Marts— begin opening during the last week of November. It doesn't matter where you are; in villages, towns, and cities, there is almost always at least one Kris Kringle Mart. It's in these markets that you can find some of the most authentic German goods, because they are all hand-made. Each of the stalls in a Kris Kringle Mart offers different things—from delicious baked goods, to toys, to fine leatherwork. By Christmas Eve, most markets will have closed down, and a few will close earlier. The history and traditions of Christmas in Germany is quite interesting. The name we often use for Santa Claus, Kris Kringle, originally evolved out of the word Christkindl, or "Christ Child." Additionally, we derive all manner of Christmas traditions from the German culture. The Adventskalender, those festive looking calendars feature a 24-day count up to Christmas disguised as windows and doors, was originally created by the Germans. As one of the Christmas customs

Germany, candles or chocolates are placed inside the paper windows as treats for children prior to Christmas. At these wonderful fairs they also sell their handmade and baked treats as well as imported and homemade lace, wooden dolls, puppets, just about anything you can imagine and all at wonderful prices. One can always count on a great schnitzel or wurst with pommes frites (French Fries) from several of the stands. Sweet treats such as stolen and plum cake or German apple cake abound and on cold days at the festivals, Glühwein, a concoction of dry red wine and spices warms the cockles of your heart.

As always I had our home decorated and everything was ready for Christmas except the tree. "Let's put it up tonight, guys…it is the fifth of December, and if I go into labor soon, best to have it up and ready!" So up went our Christmas Tree, and that night, during the wee hours of the morning, I felt the first stirrings of pain that heralded the onset of hard labor. "Art, Art wake up. I am in labor. We have to go! Oh I hope the car starts. "We had become accustomed to having Art take the car up to the top of the parking lot to get a running start, and then I would jump in at the front door. Everything was all right as long as we did not have to stop. So, as was the custom on this very cold night in December, we said a quick prayer, crossed our fingers, called the babysitter, and I managed to get into the car as it moved past the entrance to our apartment. The drive was a frightening one. The roads were slick and icy due to a snowfall the previous day, and we could only hope that we would make it to Landstuhl without having to stop the car. In the pre-dawn hours, we saw the hospital before us and gave a quick prayer of thanks that we had made it without a problem. Just as we pulled into the parking lot, the car gave a final whimper, snort, and then died. We were on foot. We had parked at the wrong entrance and were trudging through knee- deep snow to the closest lit entrance we could find. "Yes, sir. Your wife is fully dilated. Time to get her ready." Before we knew it, I was laying on a table in the delivery room giving birth to a healthy baby boy. "It's a boy, Jan. This time, it's a boy!" Smiles from the attending nurses and delivery doctor greeted me as I tried to raise my head to get a glimpse of our son. "What will you name him?" We had not settled on a name. The doctor laughed. "Well, you have to name him Nicholas, of course. Today is St Nicholas Day!" And so, of course, *Nicholas* it was!

St. Nicholas Day, or Eve, is celebrated on December 6. This is the favorite holiday of all children - it's a gift-giving day. When evening comes, St. Nicholas, a reverend gray-haired figure with flowing beard, wearing gorgeous bishop's garments, gold embroidered cope, mitre and pastoral staff, knocks on doors and enquires about the behavior of the children. The custom of examining the children, where they will cite a verse, sing, or otherwise show their skills, is still widespread in German-speaking countries. Each little one gets a gift for his performance.

The story of St. Nicholas, the bishop of Myra in Minor Asia, who died on December 6th, 343, dates back to the 4th century. He is said to appear in the company of Knecht Ruprecht, "Knecht" meaning "servant." Historically, Ruprecht was a dark and sinister figure wearing a tattered robe with a big sack on his back in which, as a legend says, he would put all naughty children. St. Nicholas also appears together with St. Peter, with an angel, the Christ child (Christkindl). As the gift-giving function of St. Nikolaus began to shift to the splendor of the candle-lit Christmas tree and emphasis on the birth of Christ, Knecht Ruprecht became the servant and companion of the Christ child. In this role Ruprecht became the patron saint of Christmas and was called "Weihnachtsmann," Father Christmas or Santa Claus.

Nicholas and I bonded immediately. He was a snuggly, happy baby who curled his little body very close to my heart. On day number five, Art was given a ride up to the hospital. Off we sped down the autostrada to our waiting daughters and a great celebration of joy. But something was wrong. The day after Christmas, Nicholas became fretful and cried often. I soon began to notice bruising around his belly button. His umbilical cord had fallen off early while I was still in the hospital. Two days after Christmas, back to Landstuhl we went. By now, the bruising had extended up his belly and he was in constant pain. After several tests, including a spinal tap, the doctors diagnosed him with a life threatening umbilical infection. He would need to stay. Every day we made the long trip back and forth to the hospital. Our neighbors took turns giving us transportation until Art could purchase another car. Oh how we wanted our son home with us for New Years. On New Year's Eve, we watched the fireworks from Nicholas's bedroom window. His little crib was empty and I held his blankets close to me. "Maybe he can come home tomorrow, Art." Sure enough, the following morning the phone rang. "He has a way to go but we feel he will be better at home with his family. You may come and get him. Just keep him on his medicine and we will see him in a week."

Off we went, back to Landstuhl to get our newborn son. He seemed to be waiting, and as I pulled his little snuggly body close to my heart, I whispered "Happy New Year, Nicholas, Happy New Year!

The Christmas Moon[5]

Kathryn Rantala

Take this peach,
it is bruised
but so fresh and cold.
It was riding a storm into winter,
a lantern afloat.
When it came to the door this morning,
we knew what it was,
and let it in.

Happy Holidays…

---

[5] *The Christmas Moon* was previously published as "The Moon" in Tundra, Issue "1, July 1999. Copyright Michael D. Welch (editor) 248 Beach Park Boulevard,Foster City

Reflective Christmas Ornaments

David Lester Young

The fire cracks aloud mellow mood soft serenity,
Christmas light dance along musical cast identity.
Christmas night chill of reflective ornament's tree
Children sleep upstairs in anticipated morning glee.

Around the evergreen lay mother's memory booty.
Heart adornment bearing the love's adoration beauty.
Father handcrafted pieces, being added in love each year.
The angel collection that sings its chorus faith, so dear.

Gift assembled sparkling glitter of parent's glimmering eyes,
Those tears that talk silently in spirit inside the heart's alter.
The prayers in reflection that bless families in celestial delight
That shares the greatest miracle of His divine celebration insight.

David Lester Young 07/28/10

Christmas Mountain

RJ Slais

On a cool crisp autumn night, I had a Christmas dream, which may seem kind of crazy since it was only late October, yet the Christmas season did arrive during my sleep that night. In this dream, I am cruising in a Christmas red Chrysler convertible, the top is down, the car is a converted convertible while I am cruising in this Christmas dream, dreaming in late October. I am cruising this dream car, a Christmas red Chrysler convertible converted up a hill, maybe even a mountain, and it sure seems like a steep mountain to climb, but not a Christmas mountain, but what the hell is a Christmas mountain anyway, but there are Christmas trees with Christmas lights going round and around them, lining the road on this hill, this mountain, so maybe it is a Christmas mountain after all.

So, as I cruise up Christmas Mountain, in my Christmas red Chrysler convertible converted surrounded by Christmas trees with Christmas lights, going round and around them, I am feeling a lot of stress. In this Christmas dream, dreaming in late October, I am stressed, in a crisis because I realize I am not climbing fast enough as Christmas Mountain is super steep and the road circles cautiously round and around only going up slightly each circle just like the rows of Christmas lights go round and around a Christmas tree. I am not cruising cautiously in my Christmas red Chrysler convertible converted as I am in a crisis. I must get up. I must get up Christmas Mountain, not get up from my Christmas dream I am dreaming in late October, so I keep Christmas dreaming and I keep cruising carelessly not cautiously and because I am in a crisis and I am cruising carelessly and not cautiously, I crash.

I crash over the cliff of Christmas Mountain, through the Christmas trees with Christmas lights that line that circling road in this Christmas dream. My Christmas red Chrysler convertible converted crashes, cascades side to side crushing the one side and then crushing the other side and even though my Christmas red Chrysler convertible is converted, I somehow remain in the car, I am contained and I remain in a crisis because I am going down Christmas Mountain not up, crashing down through Christmas trees with Christmas lights going round and around them, crushing the sides of my Christmas red Chrysler convertible. I realize that I am in a crisis in this Christmas dream because in my Christmas dream, it is the day before Christmas and I realize that I have not completed any Christmas shopping yet. I realize that I may have missed the chance to purchase my sister Christine's Christmas present and my sister Christine loves Christmas, she loves Christmas presents and Christmas trees and Christmas lights.

The more I dream, the more Christmas Mountain conquers me. I constantly crash my Christmas red Chrysler convertible converted over the cliffs through Christmas trees with Christmas lights going round and around them, cruising back up and crashing back down Christmas Mountain and now I have finally realized exactly why I am in a crisis in this Christmas dream, dreaming in late October because I have not purchased my sister Christine's Christmas present so I am not driving cautiously in my now crushed Christmas red Chrysler convertible converted. All this stress and crisis created by my Christmas dream, crashing constantly down Christmas Mountain on the day before Christmas through Christmas trees with Christmas lights going round and around them, in my now crushed Christmas red Chrysler convertible converted wanting only to purchase my sister

Christine's Christmas present because my sister Christine loves Christmas, Christmas presents, Christmas trees, and Christmas lights, finally awakens me.

My Christmas dream has ended and I am finally up and I realize that it is not Christmas yet. I realize it is only late October. I realize what I must do and I realize that to do it I must get dressed first. So I get dressed, putting on my blue jeans, my blue tee shirt, my blue sweater, my blue socks, my blue shoes, and finally my blue jacket. I go outside into the late October chill and get into my blue truck to cruise to the shopping center. It being late October, there is no sunshine outside. The sky, covered by cold clouds, is blue-brown. I cruise to the shopping center on straight streets that are slicked with brown mud. Surrounding the streets, the sleeping grasses have turned brown, the brown leaves have fallen off the brown trees and they now gather in brown piles on the brown grasses, and they swirl round and around the sides of the straight streets slicked with brown mud.

I finally enter the shopping center still remembering the resolve I carry caused by my Christmas dream. I must purchase my sister Christine at least one Christmas present. Finally, I find the perfect present sitting on a small shelf, a small shelf sitting right next to summer's seldom used clearance sale sales. I will buy my sister Christine a snow globe, a crystal snow globe with a Christmas scene inside. A Christmas scene of a Christmas mountain covered by Christmas trees that have Christmas lights going round and around them. I shake it once and let it settle. The snow falling inside sure looks like something one might see in a dream.

Lamb

Mary Barnet

Fear of far travel
Yields to Creation :
Whispered bleating of a lamb
For the Lamb
Comes to lead the way ;
Awe within the booming of the cosmos.
The little men all about -
A star blooming in the reaches of sky
Scatters everywhere to the Son
Betwixt desert and mountains ;
So dawn find herself reborn : the sun
Finds an infant
Seed of the world
Caressing by and for
All.

"Nativity" by Richard E. Schiff

The Jesus I Knew

Santosh Kumar

I thank God for the honesty and virility of Jesus religion which makes us face the facts and calls us to take a man's part in the real battle of life.
—Henry Van Dyke

i.
Shielding eyes with His grace
Staying close to Him
Disarm angry devil
Stolen by Satan
Soul-retrieval
With Jesus

ii.
Unlocked gate:
A few deep breaths with Prayer
Reaching the top
Casting off mud

Forgetting scratch marks
Starting at zero
I pray

iii.
twin towers fell
Ocean of tears
Breach in nature
Boundless darkness.
Refilling the mind with
Ten Commandments
Shanti Shanti[6]
Golden age revisits the earth

---

[6] Note: Shanti is Peace that transcends understanding.

The Christmas Train

Jill Lane

Everyone has a favorite holiday memory, and I am no exception. Mine however, doesn't revolve around a special gift…or a holiday homecoming… or personal experience, but rather another family's holiday miracle of sorts.

Christmas, as we all know, is magical in the eyes of children. The wonder of the season is nothing less than joy and expectation. Add to this holiday recipe a special *Christmas Train* and an encounter with Santa Claus…well, what's not to be magical for the little ones.

In Chama, we have a train…a very wonderful old-time steam train that chugs over narrow gauge rails high into the mountains. Through the summer and autumn seasons, our train takes visitors from all parts of the world on a ride back into time, amidst spectacular scenery in the magnificent Rocky Mountains.

As autumn leaves drop and snow begins to blanket the mountains, the train pulls up its covers for a well-deserved winter's rest, BUT not before it takes folks on one more magical ride into the mountains aboard the family oriented *Christmas Train*.

In 2004, we had our very first *Christmas Train* in many years. Everyone was excited about it… kids and adults alike. The train sold out well in advance of the actual date…and anticipation only grew as each day brought holiday riders to the highly anticipated day.

The night before the Train ride, holiday families arrived in Chama decked out in red sweaters, holiday parkas and even snow gear for the little ones. "Would there be snow on THE day?" asked all the children. "Will Santa be on the train too?" "Will the Train be fun?" Everyone happily prepared for the special *Christmas Train* the next day.

The world awoke that Saturday morning to a vision out of a fairy tale. Snow had blanketed the world in gentle, soft beauty turned Christmas Fantasy Land. The excitement rose with the tick of every minute on the clock….now the time was drawing near for the *Christmas Train*.

Ready for their magical day to begin, folks eagerly gathered at the Chama Depot. The historic yellow Depot was draped with garlands of pine boughs and red ribbons. There was a Bonfire in the Station yard, crackling flames billowing up into the sky and cheery Christmas music emanating from inside the Depot. Cookies and cocoa helped pass the time as the visitors, tucked in their snow parkas, boots and gloves, all took in this old-fashioned setting.

Finally, it was time to board the Train. Each train car had a Story Teller. Since I had written the story "Cinder Bear and the Christmas Train" soon to be read on board the train, I was one of the storytellers. We didn't want to replicate other holiday trains that were all reading the popular *Polar Express*. Instead, we would have our very own story, taking place on our very own train with the Train's mascot, Cinder Bear.

Folks, big and small all found their way to their assigned seats. The Story Tellers on each car explained the schedule. "Welcome everyone to the 1st Christmas Train…in a long, long time! We are so glad to have you on board with us today…and we hope you find this train ride a magical holiday experience that you won't soon forget."

"Shortly you will hear the blast of the Train Whistle. That first whistle tells us it is story time. So when you hear that first whistle, please sit quietly and listen as you learn all about Cinder Bear's special Train ride on this very same train! We do hope you like the story!"

"Once the story is over . . . you will hear another whistle. This second whistle means we are pulling out of the station for our ride. You can move around the train, visit with other kids and families, enjoy cocoa and cookies in the Concession car…and take in the snowy mountain world we will be riding through on the train trip. BUT . . . and listen closely now . . ."

"When the Train STOPS . . . run back to your seat and look out the window! You might just see some special guests ready to board the train and ride back with us! And who do you think those special guests might be?"

The children all cried out in unison "Santa Claus?" "Cinder Bear?" . . . and the Storyteller just shook her head and said, "You'll just have to wait and see."

Shortly thereafter, the whistle sounded and each Storyteller began to read: "Once upon a time . . ." and all eyes and ears of the children, their moms, dads, and grandparents were glued to the Storyteller.

Once the story was read, the second whistle sounded and the familiar and popular chug-chug-chug of the train began as the old steam train pulled out of the station, making its way along the silvery tracks winding through the mountains. Everyone enjoyed the camaraderie on board this special train ride. Youngsters delighted in the steamy hot cocoa and sweet treats and the oldsters took in the beauty of the winter scenery along with the magic of this holiday train ride so visible in the little ones eyes and happy smiles.

Now that the story was over and the train ride was in full gear, I had a chance to observe the passengers on my car. I saw 3 generations of happy families laughing and engaging in this holiday experience.

However, one family stood out. They were a nice looking group…three generations, obviously, but a bit unusual. Sort of a 'mix-match family.' There was a Grandmother figure-the Matriarch of the clan, and the two parents in their late 20s, a nice looking Caucasian couple…and 4 children ranging in age from a baby of about 18 months up to a 10 year old.

But what made them stand out were their physical differences. The oldest boy, around 10 was dark haired, dark-skinned with Hispanic features, very unlike his parents. The next child in size and age was a little girl about 5 years old with fair skin, curly blonde hair and blue eyes, very different from her older brother. The third child was a little boy about her same age and size who had bright red hair, lots of freckles and a devilish All-American boy look. The youngest child, the toddler was a sweet looking, little girl, with big, brown eyes, dark hair and skin, who closely resembled the oldest boy in the family.

As I observed 'my mix-match family', I noticed that they stood out, not just in their physical differences, but also in the children's actions. While most of the children on the train were running back and forth, with treats in hand, and beckoning their parents in loud, joyful antics, these four children sat quietly by their parents and grandmother, watching everything with big eyes and wonderment. They almost clung to the adults.

I wondered at their quietness in this happy festive time. They didn't look unhappy, they just emanated a calm quiet, unusual to children in this holiday scene.

My ruminations over this family were cut short as the next train whistle sounded and the chug-chug-chug of the train slowed to a stop. All the children raced to the windows and squealed in delight as they spotted Santa Claus and Cinder Bear waiting at the Train Crossing. And just as they had been instructed before the ride, they all raced back to their chairs, eagerly awaiting their personal visit from Santa and Cinder Bear, now boarding the train.

"HO-HO-HO! MERRY CHRISTMAS!" was heard throughout as Santa boarded the train with Cinder Bear at his side. To the delight of all, they made their way through the various cars, visiting with the children, passing out treats and taking pictures with the excited kids.

As Santa and Cinder made their way to "my mix-match family", I once again observed the difference in these four youngsters. There was no jumping up and down, shouting out to Santa Claus and clamoring to get their treats. They each sat quietly in their seat, with the littlest girl clinging to her grandmother. All four of them awaited Santa and Cinder with eyes bigger than saucers. And when Santa and Cinder got to them, they all politely accepted their gift with a softly uttered "Thank you Santa." The littlest of the four, hiding behind her Grandmother's shoulder, watched Santa and Cinder Bear in total amazement and followed their every move with her big brown eyes.

Santa and Cinder continued through the train, 'til all had been visited on the return ride. As the train arrived back at the Depot and sounded its final whistle, it chug-chug-chugged, slowing down on its final approach. The brakes squealed as the train came to a halt. The Conductor opened the doors, and the families all climbed happily down from the train cars, their holiday train ride complete.

I waited for everyone on my car to de-board, and the last ones to leave were "my mix-match family". The children, just as during the ride, politely waited their turn and then exited the train car one at a time, but not before each one of them came up to me, "Thank you Ma'am, this was a very nice Christmas Train". The biggest boy first, with the red-headed boy and the blonde little girl mimicking his same words, and finally the littlest one just reached out to me and gave me a soft little hug . . .her eyes still large with wonderment at the entire experience.

The last one off was the Grandmother. She started to descend the train steps, then turned back around, came up to me and shared with me . . . words that still ring clear in my memory.

"Thank you for this wonderful holiday experience. These children will NOT forget this train ride . . . *ever*, I'm sure. You see, these children have all four come into our family just one month ago…from several foster families. They have had a rough start to life, all had been removed from violent or sad backgrounds, and our family was lucky enough to be able to adopt them last month. None of these four children had ever experienced Christmas joy…until today. And yes, today they did witness the joy of the holidays that all children should experience. It's been a day filled with wonder for each of them . . . and for us as well."

With tears in her eyes, she gave me a quick hug, turned around and descended the train's steps. With a final wave to me, the family disappeared into the crowd of happy holiday revelers.

I don't know where this special family came from, and I have never seen them since, but their love and wonderment at this, the children's first ever real holiday experience, has forever stayed in my heart. This memory is one of the greatest gifts I ever received….and all because of a special *Christmas Train*.

"The Fir Burns" by Terri French

"Kirche im Algau" by Janet K. Brennan[7]

---

[7] "Kirche im Algau was previously published in *Taj Majal Review*, 2008

"Snowy Island", Sarasota, Florida by Peggie Devan

"Wreaths" Maine by Patricia Saunders

"Ice Trees" Norway by Mia Alexandra Oelnes

"Ice Cabin"Norway by Mia Alexandra Oelnes

"Nativity" by Richard E. Schiff

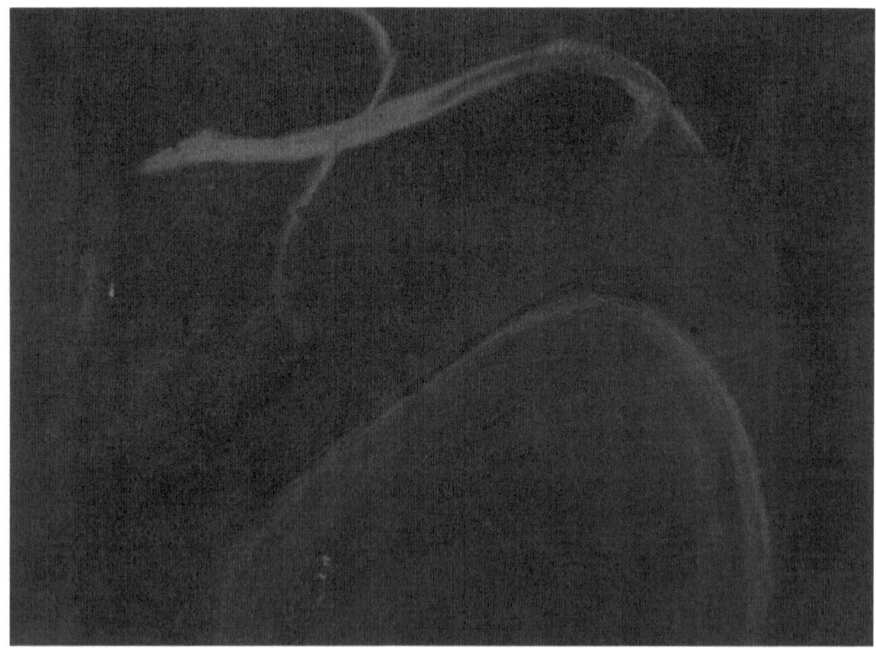

"Calalilly" by Kate Luke

"A Rose in Winter" New Mexico by Janet K. Brennan

"Holiday Tree" by Patricia Saunders

"San Felipe de Neri Church" Albuquerque by Art Brennan

"Gracie's Dream" by Janet K. Brennan

A Chanukah Song

Charles Adès Fishman

Back then, it was *O
Holy Night* we thrilled
to. The gymnasium was filled
with high childish voices
and that one note rose,
like a flaring star, a full
octave above us: it was your
voice, David. You were fourteen
or eleven — I can't remember —
and you chilled us to the bone.
But I could not sing *by heart*
what we mouthed together. Oh,
how I might have been lifted
had your savior been my own!
Remember my try-out for chorus:
Adeste Fidelis . . . my voice
breaking on "Chri-ist, the Lord!"

This night, the choir sings,
in near-perfect Hebrew, a Chanukah
song, and — though Bach's *O Beauteous
Heavenly Light* does indeed break forth
from these girls and boys, our children —
it is this shard of Jewish life that moves me
to rejoice.

Christmas Glow

Janet Yaeger

Ice covered trees with blankets of snow
Cozy retreats inside homes all aglow
Fireplaces warming hearts, warming hands
Christmas is here and it's time once again…

To gather together, the young and the old,
Families united, old stories retold.
Remembering loved ones who no longer share
Another Christmas with loved ones this year.

Sweet, fragrant aromas from kitchens complete
With big country tables set, ready to feed
Grandpa, Nana, Mother and Dad,
From the tiny new baby to big Uncle Fred.

Christmas is here; all are full of good cheer.
How did it get here so fast this year?
Opening presents that barely got wrapped.
Dad wondering how bad the checkbook got zapped.

Afternoon spent playing games, taking naps,
Some reminisce and others share laughs.
Cleaning up dishes and paper and boxes.
Listing to Uncle Fred being obnoxious.

Christmas has gone by, so quickly it seems
That it's already part of our past Christmas dreams.
Relatives gone, children nestled in bed.
The once noisy house is now quiet, instead.

Christmas has come, now it's over again.
Once warmed by the fire; now we're warmed from within.
We go to bed, our souls all aglow
In our home, our cozy retreat from the snow.

Christmas in the Last Century

Lynn Strongin

What kept each of us alive? Music for Rachel: for Mother, her two daughters'; for me, writing and the ongoing struggle of rehabilitation. If one took these away, we would die. I knew there was nothing to do but surrender to the wave immense and green, washing over me, the words rolled as in as from the green ocean. I wrote, the gift at last I recognized it as which carried me away. It was stronger, bigger than me.

If wishes were horses, beggars might ride. Thus, I rode my buckskin pony with the blue zigzag neon eyes.

O thread-thin smocks from my cousin! O box of white balloons Mother finally shoved bitterly one day in the bin, on walking on water which I'd never do again. Alzora Hightower and that shimmering feeling I got in bed with Skippy, night-things with which I am in love, never be gone.

To surrender means, among other things, to relinquish possession, to abandon hope. I did neither--or did I? Did Charlotte do it once and for our family? *I will save my skin.*

Coda

Goodnight, Alzora Hightower, you are forgiven, Goodnight, Chad Livingood. Good night, Skippy. Sleep well, Matthew Countryman. We are sourced. Nothing can unsource us for good. LaTour shadows in this room, I blow the candle out.. Skippy, May your rickets back unbend in heaven. Lord, unfold me, uncomplicate, and let me be shorn of all frill and ornament. Have I reached forgiveness of myself? I wake pauper and king. All that has been taken, all given, no sacrifice, but survival—still like a beggar, I surrender, and surrendering ride, (with Skippy, with Rachel, with Charlotte, with Mother) wish-horses who plunge into the foam leaving only the tracery of words, like love's transition, from desire to embrace to release, love at last becoming like pewter sky in winter, or December sea, sheer endurance. The unbending ways of God. To surrender is to turn over, but to turn over *something*, not to surrender the self, *not to succumb.*

*

I don't sacrifice or surrender, but simply exchange: so here are my cotton dresses for the brand-new ones. Here is meditation in place of walking. Here is a rule of thumb in place of revelation. I forgive what I have forfeited. It has been a hard forging but having gone thru the fire, the dross is burned off: it is pure gold.

Will there flash a later, darker epiphany? What happened to me to change my life happened when I was twelve years of age. There was no question of anger or forgiveness then. Only survival was at stake. Now at seventy, forgiveness is foremost and almost accomplished. Those beggar's horses are sea horses who ride sea-waves, green, becoming a bright dissolving signature of ocean, which crashes, and surrenders, leaving its story, its tragedy, its passions written first in water, then like the wave breaking upon cliff, at last dissolving when it strikes hard cliff.

Happy Chanukah

Untitled

Lee Hepworth

It is upon us, the longest night--
and yet I have not confused my mind
as I watch the masters turn to
servants — and women into wine'
for all shall be so different this day--
be it of the turning zodiac, to that
of virtues sang — the prison is broken
for the king, and reached out furthest
to return reborn, the sun.

I think of forgiveness this day,
for even Hades sits within what he
was without, his home, in the heavens,
for this day all is forgotten and brought
back anew.

Come people sing, dance,
as everyone down the centuries did before,
feel and be historical — as this snow-white world
has come to being; light your flames up high
and drown away the dark — hang your lanterns in
the trees; hold this year hostage, and when he shows
his face ablaze — it has come to pass.

First was the shortest day,
and my beloved friends I thank thee--
hoping that you live in peace,
this year, every year, I welcome
the sun.

Christmas in New Mexico

Frances Fanning

Like the Magi we traveled
From the East we did go
Charting the star of our dreams
To New Mexico

She was swaddled in blankets
Of new fallen snow
And we looked on in wonder
At New Mexico

We had few gifts to give her
But our hearts were aglow
With loving and caring
For New Mexico

From up on the rooftops
To the streets down below
She was covered in candles
Our New Mexico

We built her a bonfire
While the winds they did blow
And we sang Christmas greetings
To New Mexico

We sang for the strangers
 Who welcomed us so
We sang of our joy here
In New Mexico

And now at each Christmas
We bend our heads low
And say prayers of thanksgiving
To New Mexico

Christmas Morning

Lisa Arnold

hush of magical morning
warmth of golden sunshine
crystal clear blue sky
blush of angel's breath
carried by winter's wind

blanket of Christmas Eve
snow falling outside window
where children are
making lopsided snowmen
and dusty snow angels

spiced pumpkin pie in oven
cinnamon scented candles burning
mother basting turkey
grandma baking cookies
daddy kissing mama
under the mistletoe

children come inside and gather
around glowing fireplace
mother gives them
hot chocolate and warm cookies
while they listen to grandpa's stories

night falls over city
the children are now asleep
beacon of light
guides Santa's sleigh
heaven's blessed angel's sing

glorious sun rises
the children rejoice in
the majestic birth of
Christmas morning

December Morning

Katrina Wallace

Rusty railings are all edged with rime
For December's sun is slow to climb
As Dawn reveals herself through frosted glass
In smoky hues across the woods and grass
Unveiling misty robes of pearly grey
In graceful folds that slowly swirl away

Under rows and rows of trees undressed
Grandly cloaked in Winter Magic's best
I wander under snow white feathered wings
So grateful for the charms that winter brings
To muddy fields and patchwork stubble hill
Lonely now in Dawn's December chill

Yet I love to live in such a place
When sunlight drapes the trees in fragile lace
Releasing Autumn's few remaining leaves
That float like silver stars to roof and eaves
And smiling now in Dawn's first blush of day
The Morning Moon meanders on his way....

May God Bless You

Tracey Brown

I received a Christmas card today
Beautifully decorated in shades of blue.
Inside the words carefully rhymed
Signed with the traditional "May God Bless You"

If they only knew the blessings
God had already bestowed on me.
They would have just sent a reminder
For me to open my eyes to see.

The beautiful sunrise He paints each morning
As I quietly sit and read His word.
The melodious tones of the morning birds
More beautiful than any orchestra I've heard.

The comfort and joy in knowing
I can go to Him with any care
And no matter what my day will bring
The assurance I have, He's always there.

The family and friends around me
That adds such richness to my life.
I know He's placed each and every one
To share my triumphs and my strife.

But the greatest blessings He's given me
Is far outmatched by anything.
Because of His love and sacrifice
One day I'll see my Lord and King.

So, I won't offer "May God Bless You'
To help celebrate this Christmas Day
Instead I'll offer just a reminder
"May you see God's blessing in each new day."

Winter Tree

Katrina K Guarascio

He says it isn't a Christmas tree,
it's a Winter Tree,
and that is why it sits in the living room till March.

I ask why all the decorations
on it look Christmassy
and have Santa, reindeer, and the rest of the crew
etched onto red and green.

He faults popular society.
If it were up to him,
Winter Tree decorations would be more universal,
but right now, he has to use what is available.

I ask him if he'll take it down on the twentieth.
Of course, he replies,
a Winter Tree can't stay up in the spring.

A Christmas Eve Proposition

Katrina K Guarascio

He says
he's no good around the holidays.
Carols irritate stomach bile,
media muddles mind,
and all the obsession with wrapping paper
makes him sick for the human race.

You agree,
this time of year etches cold on your bones.
You hear it in the obligatory chime of church bells,
see it in expectations dressed in ribbon and money clips.

You lack the adequacy of gift giving and small talk,
and wake up so often alone on Christmas morning
it's become the only way you know.

He says,
that shade of jade looks good on you,
but he'd rather see you wearing his lips,
and perhaps waking up in each other's arms
can rekindle an excitement for a holiday morning
inexperienced since childhood.

You suggest
creamed coffee and furry slippers,
the classic Star Wars trilogy on local cable
while nestling under down comforter
and breakfasting on easy bake cinnamon rolls,
the kind Mom used to leave in the freezer.

He says,
he doesn't mind the commercials
or waiting for the oven to ring because
it gives him time to untie your bow
and unwrap the only gift you have to give.

You say,
you can't think of a better way to make merry
than folded up in him.

He says,
We're not made to spend the day submerged in strangers.
Instead, create a new tradition, exclusive to two,
the only exchange: the warmth between bodies,
the only holiday: an unhurried moment,
the only commitment: an epiphany of peace.

Time

Kairawan Joseph

Today is now, yesterday is gone, tomorrow has 24 hours in its day,
The future, my friend, is not very far it's merely seconds away.

∞

That which we cannot hold is time, no matter how hard we try.
Time can be our enemy or friend, depending on its generosity.
For you see, although we cannot control time, it does not have to control us.
Time's controlling power surges when we dwell on the past or get stuck on today.

∞

Time is always moving, so must we,
Refuse the trap of stagnancy.

Go on and live — Go ahead be bold!
Now you've overcome time — The future is yours to hold.

Portland, Isle of Slingers

Andrew Shiston

Come to this island, the land of Slingers
dark cliffs above the Pousidedon's sea
the bay of shingle, inlets like fingers
on the shore of England land of the free
hear folklore from the Portland Bill singers
see fossilised stools, branches of a tree
see Norman churches, hear the bell ringers
visit the old harbour sat in the lee
smell the ozone that often lingers
after sou-sou-west storms, that does flee
taste the Spider Crab that Portland brings us
food from the sea I'm sure you will agree

Jurrasica coast cliffs on Dorset's land
deposited hear by God's open hand.

Haiku

Terri French & Michelle Hed

winter sky
Alcyone outshines
her sisters

bare birch limbs
I think of all the gloves
I've lost

magnolia and cedar
share the mantle
our backsides share the fire

deep in douglas fir
the woodpecker and I
listening

winter circles the house
nudging its chill
beneath the door

blowing into
my cupped hands--
the last leaf falls

clumps of mistletoe
in bare branches--
so many unkissed lips

long winter
dreaming of
tomatoes

silent night--
my distorted face
in the Christmas ball

fresh snow--
steam rises
from the newborn calf

lone goose
at beaver's pond--
a gap in the "v"

 Festival Day

Aiswarya T Anish
Age 14

I smile as the light falls on my face,
Jump back, turn around, the curtains I raise
I view the world with a surprised eye
I remember the day with a joyous sigh

It's mid-summer, mid-spring, with a little heat
I jump up and down, as if I've spring-clad feet
It is Festival Day, the best time of the year
I sing with the cuckoo, so beautiful, so clear

It's harvest time, the fields' gold with grain
Its happy times, forget the ones with pain
Just sing out loud, like the birds and the beasts
Sing out loud as you lay out the feasts

It's green in the woods and blue in the skies
The people rainbow as they slash out the rice
There's no more tears, no more wails
Happiness shown in so many details

It's the New Year, here, calls the red birds
The fun can't be said, in just little words
It is true, that this time is the best
East or west, Festival Day is the best!

12th January 2011
Aishu is 14 from Kerala India

Old Maude

Jon Hovis

Edwin Armstrong drew a long whistling breath through his clay pipe as he considered the snow blowing around him. The cold didn't bother him much, it was the wind. The wind made for some awful conditions up on the mountain, and most likely, there would be more snowdrifts to clear. Looking with disgust at the pipe as it went out again, Edwin tapped out the ashes and headed inside his little two room cottage.

Little Emily smiled up at her father as he entered the room, "Is it gonna be a blizzard?" she asked innocently, "there has to be snow for Santa's sled, you know."

"Don't you worry about it, Pumpkin; Santa always finds a way through." Edwin didn't let his worry show; he was confident that his snowplow could make it up to the pass, he just wasn't sure that he could do it before Christmas Eve, which was only three days away. The last train in from Denver had been turned back due to the weather, and now this new storm threatened to strand the small town of Chama, New Mexico. Emily had enough problems since she had lost her mother the year before, what with trouble in school and being raised by just her dad. Now, the only present that she wanted, a doll made in Paris, was on that train . . . *along with supplies for the whole town*, he thought. "Well, off to bed, child, it's going to be an early morning for both of us."

Emily had just kissed her father goodnight when heavy footsteps could be heard outside. Getting up from his chair, Edwin opened the door to find one of the yard hands stomping snow from his boots. "What's happening?" he asked, already knowing the answer.

"Just got word, Chief. The night train was stuck in a snowdrift just this side of Cumbres Pass. There are passengers on that train so we've gotta move; lives are at risk!"

"All right, I'll be right along." Edwin forced the door shut against the wind and turned to find Emily holding his coat and boots. He gave a brief smile as he considered this young girl. Forced to grow up too fast in the past year, she was still a girl trying to act like an adult. *But she still wants a doll for Christmas.* He gave her instructions to keep the fire going as he pulled on his boots. "I don't know how long I'll be, so don't leave the house."

"Okay, Chief," she liked to call him that when he ordered her about.

Edwin scowled at her as he pecked the top of her head and tromped out the door. He certainly knew how to order his men around. He was plain spoken and stern, but he was fair and the men knew it. They would follow him to hell and back if it was called for; he was just that kind of leader. They also knew that he had a soft spot for his daughter and respected him for it.

Edwin strained to see through the snowflakes as he walked up behind his men. "Just another winter in Chama, year 1926," Edwin joked with his fireman as he inspected "Old Maude", a rotary snowplow. A pilot and qualified locomotive engineer, Edwin had been running the OM for ten years now. The wheelman and fireman had already been on site, and had the boiler stoked and ready to go. Edwin, as the pilot, acted as chief engineer and directed the entire operation. Four 2-8-0 Baldwin locomotives would be used to push the steam powered snowplow up to and through the snowdrifts. The length of time required to clear the tracks depended on the depth of the snow and how much track was blocked.

The Chama rail yard was a flurry of activity as a small 0-6-0 yard engine moved in a water tank car behind the OM, while each Baldwin ran under the coal chute for a full load. Each locomotive had to be oiled and inspected, while the firemen threw in shovelfuls of coal into the firebox. Smoke and cinders filled the air, mixing with the snow, making it difficult to see. Every man knew his job and the operation came together quickly. By the time daybreak arrived, the train was assembled and ready to roll.

Edwin waited for the yard engine to roll past, cross the turntable, and take cover inside the roundhouse. With the tracks clear, he sounded two long blasts of the whistle signaling for the locomotive engineers to open it up. Even though visibility was bad, he knew these tracks so well he could tell just by feel where they were. The snowplow train soon hit top speed and raced up the mountain towards the high country and the stranded train.

Cold and hot at the same time, Chief Engineer Edwin Armstrong pulled his head back inside as he signaled with the whistle for the locomotives to slow. A corner was coming up and he couldn't see more than fifty feet. A blast from the open fire grate quickly warmed him back up as the fireman threw in shovelfuls of coal. They were getting close and it was time to get the plow ready to work.

Suddenly, there it was! Just past Windy Point, a wall of snow covered the tracks for as far as he could see. Edwin grabbed the whistle and signaled the stop. He ordered the wheelman to climb out on top of the rotary to see how far the drift extended. When the man was outside, Edwin whistled a warning signal, one long and one short blast, to see if the stranded locomotive was in reach. After a second there was a short, two blast reply. The stranded train was within earshot, but well over one hundred feet of deep snow blocked the way.

The wheelman leaned down from the roof and stuck his head in the window, "She's over there all right! Steam's still up and she's alive, but the snow is up to the light. We're gonna have a time of it!"

"Well, all right then; get inside and let's get at it." Edwin engaged the plow and pulled the throttle. Steam power started to rotate the huge plow and he signaled for the four locomotives behind to start pushing. The chief engineer calmly gave orders as needed as the men started work. It would take hours but they had to get the stuck train and its passengers to safety. "Keep the pressure up," he told the fireman. "Put the downhill side flange down," he told the wheelman, "We need to keep the snow away from the sides as well."

As Old Maude pushed into the snowdrift, the rotary plow ate away at the pile and flung it off to the side. The men positioned the chute so the wind carried away the snow. After several feet, the locomotives started to slip and they had to stop and try again. With each push they would get through several feet of snow and then have to repeat the process. They worked for hours, pushing and pulling, re-adjusting the side flange and the discharge chute. Edwin ran the whole show, signaling for the locomotives to change direction, push harder, or slack off. Slowly, foot by foot, they made progress. Towards the middle of the drift, the snow was higher than the OM, slowing their advance. They would have to hit the snow as much as possible and then back off as the snow above the level of the plow collapsed. Then they could move forward and clear again.

Now, with the deepest part cleared, progress was picking up. The chief signaled for a little more power out of the locomotives and the men poured it on. With just the right amount of power behind the rotary, Old Maude churned her way through and soon they had reached the stranded train.

Passengers from the train cheered as their rescuers arrived. It was nearly dark, having taken the crew all day to bust through. The rotary snowplow was covered in snow and the men were exhausted, but they found a new burst of energy as they accomplished their monumental task.

Wasting little time, Edwin ordered the plow team to reverse and head back down the mountain. Shortly thereafter, the stranded train followed and they all headed back to Chama. Edwin allowed himself a small, half smile as he thought about how well his team handled the snowdrift and just a little bit of pride in Old Maude for knocking out another one.

On the following evening, Edwin sat in his chair, feet up to the fire, and chewed on his unlit pipe. Emily could hardly contain herself after they had returned from the Christmas Eve church service. There was a package next to the fireplace. "Did Santa come?" she asked. She was old enough to know better but still young enough to pretend.

"I don't know," her father answered, "Perhaps we can open it in the morning…"

"No!"

Edwin laughed out loud. "Go ahead," he allowed, "I think you'll like it."

Too Much Snow

Lola R. Eagle

The snow came on this Christmas-tide,
More than we'd ever seen.
The mountains, cacti, it did hide
With white so heavenly clean.

Blanketing the land around,
It looked fantastic thus.
Yet on it came down to the ground,
Grew high, then formed a crust.

At first the scene before our eyes
Uplifted all who saw,
But purity of snowflakes dies
When piled in every draw.

Our startled senses soon grew numb
From watching banks of snow,
As on it fell in silence from
The heavens to earth below.

It seemed a never-ending thrall
Of beauty from the skies,
But those of us who watched it fall
 Lost interest by and by.

For hours and hours the stuff came down;
How much is left up there?
Let's share it with another town
And save some for next year.

HalloGivingMas

Lola R. Eagle

Well, here it is almost Halloween, and I have to put my blinders on whenever I go to shop so that I am not side-tracked from my Thanksgiving preparations by Christmas ornaments.

Sometime along about August or the early part of September, I throw a few bags of Halloween candy in my shopping cart and wonder idly about black cat cutouts for the living room window and orange-colored leaf bags to simulate jack-o-lanterns on the lawn.

However, before I get around to those All-Hallowed Eve decorations, I'm hit with little Pilgrim candles, cornucopia and gourds exhorting me to make "darling centerpieces" for our Thanksgiving table.

So I begin to dig through the closet in search of my three-size, stuffed-felt pumpkin set, thinking perhaps I am behind schedule.

Long, l-o-n-g before December, the stores transform themselves into silvery tinsel-towns and there is no getting past the angels, bells, lit-up ceramic villages, plastic trees, and old-world Santas.

Then it is I try to remember – is this October, Novober, or Devember. Still August? No way!

I'm lost in a speeded-up fall, never quite sure what month or day it is.

How do those Madison Avenue ad-men expect us to buy all the touted nimiety of each holiday when they don't give us time to look at it, let alone consider it, before they glut the market with the next holiday's trappings, and the next after that. We are besieged with the superfluity of every holiday all at once. They are doing themselves in!

The first glimpse of the shiny distractions causes us to take pause. "Maybe that would look nice in my living room." Our next walk-through elicits the thought, "I believe I have something like that in the attic."

After weeks and weeks of passing these displays of snow-filled scenes, listening to Santa snore in his rocking chair and humming along with the tinkling bells, we lose interest. After all, it's time now to turn our attention to our gift list. Didn't that sign just inform us there are only 72 shopping days until Christmas? We can't be bothered any more with thinking about Halloween pumpkins, Thanksgiving cornucopia, or even Christmas angels. We have to shop, shop, shop! New Year's Eve is coming, and it's almost Valentine's Day!

Happy Fourth of JuChristmas!

A Family Tradition

Lola R. Eagle

All these many years later, I am still making Christmas coffee cakes. I have often pleaded with my family, "Forget the coffee cakes this year!" But I'm not allowed to forget, for they have become our family tradition.

On Easter Sunday, the year I was married, someone brought this "pull-apart" cake as a treat for our church choir to enjoy between services. Made of dozens of small balls of dough, dipped in melted butter and rolled in cinnamon, sugar and nuts, with raisins tucked in between the rolls, it was delicious. Everybody raved about it; many of us asked for the recipe.

At Christmas time, I decided the coffee cake would be perfect for Christmas breakfast. My husband loved it (although he picked out the raisins) and asked why I didn't make it more often. I said, "Well, it's a lot of work – all those little balls of dough…"

The next year, my husband suggested another "Christmas cake." "I'll help," he said. "We can make extras for gifts."

The next year, my husband *assumed* we would have our special Christmas treat. Well, I thought, it's only once a year.

As our children came along, they helped, too. When the fluted Bundt pans were brought out, they knew Christmas was near.

During the lonely Christmas my husband spent in Korea, he found a carefully packed coffee cake in his package from home. One year when I was ill, our 16-year-old son laboriously mixed the dough and rolled the balls, spending hours on the project. When our children left home, Christmas brought them foil-wrapped coffee cakes.

We've given those cakes to relatives, neighbors, office associates, bosses, friends – anyone with whom we wanted to share something special during the holidays. One year we made thirteen; most years we make about half a dozen. Some years they're better than other years – the dough is lighter, the baking time calculated just right.

Those cakes symbolize the holiday season for my family. Christmas wouldn't be Christmas without them. Every year they're with us.

And every year everyone but Mom picks out the raisins and leaves them on the plate!

Please Santa, Give ME a Break!

Lola R. Eagle

Christmas comes but once a year,
And now it's very near, I fear.
My trepidation comes because
I'm not prepared for Mr. Claus.

First I list my loved ones dear,
Keeping bent a hopeful ear
For helpful hints that I might use
To show me just which gift to choose.

Then, scrutinizing checkbook balance,
Finding time for daytime dalliance;
Dogged traipse through Mall and shop,
Walking, looking 'til I drop.

Watching prices skyward billow;
Wishing my feet were on a pillow.
Digging into shrinking purse;
Settling for tacky things, and worse!

I'm sure you know just how it goes
The way the Season brings its woes
Enthusiastic expectation
Evolves in time to tired frustration.

Ah, Christmas Time!
So full of cheer.
I'm glad you come
But once a year!

Never Alone

D. Allen Jenkins

"Grandpa Zeb, tell us a story!" Ten year-old Allie ran up to the side of the rocking chair. Four other grandchildren, ranging in age from four to ten, followed in her pathway and eagerly encouraged their grandpa to accept their sibling's request.

Zebediah Jennings peered over the top of his reading glasses and studied the looks of anticipation in the eyes of his family's newest generation. "Well, then," he said with a mischievous grin on the corner of his mouth, "what kind of a story would you like to hear?"

"A Christmas one." Allie quickly responded with her hands on her hips. "It is Christmas Eve after all."

"A real make-believe story Grandpa," chimed in Alex, the oldest boy of the group.

"And one about angels!" Sarah, the next oldest, added with excitement.

Grandpa Zeb nodded in acknowledgement of these suggestions, while turning toward the two youngest children. "And what about the twins," he asked, "what do you want to hear a story about?"

Four year-old David and Derrick looked at each other before David ducked behind his twin and pushed him toward the chair, as if to say *you answer him*. Derrick stumbled forward into his sister Sarah.

"How about a scaredy-cat brother." Derrick said.

"Derrick Jennings!" snapped an older female voice from the other side of the room.

"But, Mom, he pushed me into Sarah." the boy protested, glaring back at his brother who had taken refuge behind his mother's legs.

"Maybe Grandpa should tell a story about a mean brother." Mrs. Jennings responded.

Grandpa Zeb smiled, and gently motioned all of his grandchildren around him. "How 'bout I tell you a story about all of those things."

"About all of them?" Allie queried.

"Oh yes, indeed, Miss Allie," Grandpa replied, "all of them."

The four grandchildren drew in close and sat down in front of their grandfather. Their parents also sat down on a nearby couch, with David, the youngest, still clinging to his mother's leg. Grandpa Zeb paused for a moment allowing the anticipation of his audience to build. He cleared his throat.

"Once upon a time, in a small town called Bethlehem, there lived a family of shepherds. Mr. and Mrs. Shepherd had five children, whose names were..."

Allie raised her hand into the air and blurted out, "I know, I know!"

"...Sneezy, Sleepy, Grumpy..." Grandpa continued.

"Grandpa!" Allie interjected annoyingly, "those are the seven dwarves. I know their real names."

"Oh really?" Grandpa responded. "What are their real names?"

"Allie, Alex, Sarah, Derrick and David!" came the authoritative answer.

"Why how did you know that, Allie Jennings?" Grandpa said. "Have you heard this story before?"

"No, Grandpa, I just knew because there were five children in the family, just like us." Allie answered proudly.

"Well, you are a very smart little girl, Allie, because that is what their names were." Grandpa said with a pat on the young girls head.

"Everyday" Grandpa continued, "the whole family would go out into the fields and take care of their sheep. It was a very big flock, and often, Mr. and Mrs. Shepherd would have to leave to go into town to sell the wool or get supplies, and when they did, they left their children in charge of watching the sheep. Now most of the time, watching sheep was very easy. In fact, it was really boring. It was so boring that Alex, the oldest boy, once made up a song about it."

Everyone looked at Alex. "How did the song go, Grandpa?" Sarah asked.

Grandpa straightened up in his chair and said, "It went something like this:

> A shepherd's life is dull
> I don't like it at all.
> You sit and watch the sheep go by
> and then you've done it all.
>
> A shepherd's life's a bore
> I can't tell you anymore
> Cause if I did, I'd fall asleep
> and I'm afraid I'd snore
>
> If you would like this life
> and think you could pay the price
> then come and take my place for me
> I'd rather find a wife!"

Everyone clapped their hands and cheered as Grandpa finished the song, but Alex said he didn't like the part about the wife.

Grandpa Zeb laughed. "Well, I think this Alex was a little bit older than you are. But give it time."

Grandpa continued his story. "So whenever their parents left them in charge, the older ones would play tricks on the younger ones to pass the time, especially the youngest boy, named David."

The other children looked over at their brother, whose eyes grew wide with wonder.

"You see, David was not only the youngest of the children, but David had another problem that made him very different from his brothers and sisters; David couldn't talk. His parents loved him very much, but his brothers and sisters were embarrassed by him, because all the other kids in town would make fun of him. They would make fun of him too, especially when their parents were gone.

Sometimes, when Alex would sing one of his songs, they would tell David 'Sing louder, we can't hear you!' Or if they were telling jokes, they would say, 'Ok David, now it's your turn to tell us a joke.' But their favorite trick was to sneak off and leave him by himself with the sheep while they ran off to play with their friends.

It hurt David when they were mean to him; especially when they teased him about not being able to sing or tell jokes. Yet he grew to like it when they would run off and leave him by himself. At least no one was making fun of him. Still, he was lonely, and prayed that God would send him a friend that would never leave him alone."

Grandpa Zeb glanced again toward David, who had moved out in front of his mother and sat down to hear the rest of the story. Grandpa Zeb smiled and winked at his youngest progeny.

"One night, Mr. and Mrs. Shepherd told the family they had to go into Bethlehem and register for the census the Roman government had ordered. They said Allie and Alex were in charge and to make sure the sheep were guarded during the night because there were many strangers in town for the census, and someone might try to steal a sheep or a goat.

After their parents left, all of the children went out to the fields to watch over the sheep. It was a very, very cold night, and soon the four older ones decided it was too cold, and told David they were going to get some fire wood and some blankets to help stay warm.

David knew they were lying, but he knew someone had to watch the sheep, so he just tried to keep from crying as his brothers and sisters ran away into the darkness. David got up and looked around for some branches to help keep his small fire going, and then wrapped his thin coat around him as tightly as he could. David looked up at the night sky, past its twinkling stars, and silently prayed his daily prayer, 'Lord, will you please send me a friend who won't leave me alone?'

About midnight, David picked up the last few branches and placed them on top of the fire. He was very cold and tired, and he drew closer to the fire as the branches made the flames grow brighter and warmer. David closed his eyes and tried to pretend he was at home in front of the fireplace with a big bowl of hot soup.

Suddenly, the fire seemed to grow very bright and warm. He opened his eyes thinking his family had actually come back with more wood and blankets, but soon realized that, though he was not alone, it was definitely not his brothers and sisters that had come to join him.

David saw a man whose clothes shined as brightly as the sun, and he seemed to be floating in the air above him. David's eyes grew wide, and he opened his mouth, but of course he couldn't scream. He covered his face with his arms, and couldn't decide if he wanted to look at the man or to run and hide. While he thought about what to do, a voice called his name. It was a kind, but strong voice. He had never heard it before, but it made him feel safe.

"David," the voice said, "don't be afraid. I have come to bring you good news: Today, in Bethlehem, the Savior has been born. He will be the friend you have been praying for, because he will never go away or leave you alone."

David uncovered his face and realized that the angel had been joined by hundreds of other angels. They were all smiling at him, and he looked at them with amazement.

Then the first angel spoke to him again. 'Go to the stables behind the town inn. You will find the baby there, wrapped in cloth and lying in a manger.'

David nodded that he understood, and as he did, the angels rose into the sky and started shouting, 'Glory to God in the highest, peace to all men on whom His favor rests.'

David watched the angels until they disappeared. He then grabbed his shepherd's staff and ran toward Bethlehem. He had never run so fast, nor felt so happy. He felt like he was flying, and soon he came to the edge of Bethlehem where the town inn was located. He ran to the back of the inn, to the cave that served as the stable for the traveler's animals. He looked closely, at first seeing nothing but several donkeys and a horse or two.

But then, as a weary looking donkey shifted its position, he saw what the angel had told him he would see. A man and a woman were sitting on the ground beside the stone feeding trough, looking at something that seemed to be moving inside of it.

David held his breath and moved toward the man and woman. The man saw David, and smiled at him, motioning him to come and see. David ran to the man's side. His wife, tired but overjoyed, nodded to David to come see for himself.

David looked into the manger. There, wrapped in cloth, was the most beautiful baby he had ever seen. Without thinking, David extended his hand to touch the infant. Suddenly, the baby's arm stretched out and his tiny hand grabbed hold of David's finger.

Tears flowed down David's face. The angels were right. David knew this baby would be his friend forever. He would never be alone again.

As David turned to leave, he was greeted by his parents, his four brothers and sisters following after them in an unhappy procession. David stopped, afraid that he was going to be in trouble for leaving the sheep. He motioned toward the stable and the kneeling parents of the newborn baby, trying to explain why he was not with the sheep.

His father knelt and placed his hands on David's shoulders. 'David, we know why you are here. A man came to us and told us he sent you here, and everything is just like he said it would be. He said you would introduce us to your new friend.'

David's face broke into a smile, and he took his mother's hand and led them into the stable to the side other manger. David pointed to the baby, whose hand again reached out and took hold of David's fingers. David's eyes filled with tears. He looked at his mother and made a gesturing motion, then looked at the baby's mother expectantly.

'He wants to know the baby's name?' Mrs. Shepherd asked.

The baby's mother smiled, and placed her hand on David's.

'His name is Jesus,' she said. 'And I can tell that he loves you.'"

"David smiled and motioned to the baby's mother, who looked to Mrs. Shepherd for an explanation.

'He wants you to know that he loves Jesus too, and he knows that Jesus will always be his friend.'

David nodded in confirmation, and then leaned over and hugged Jesus as best he could.

I love you, Jesus, he thought, wishing he could say it with his own voice. Just then, the baby seemed to giggle. Jesus' mother smiled, 'I think he knows what you are saying to him,' she said.

David smiled in return as he took his own mother's hand. Mr. Shepherd motioned to his other four children that it was time to go home. Their faces dropped, knowing what lay ahead of them, but David's face was beaming with happiness over all that had happened that night. It didn't matter what his brothers and sisters did or said to him anymore, he had a friend who would never leave him alone. The End!"

Grandpa Zeb smiled at his enraptured grandchildren. "So did that story have everything in it?"

His audience all nodded that it did, but David ran up and grabbed hold of his grandfather's leg. "That was the best story ever, Grandpa," he exclaimed. "But what happened to David's brothers and sisters?"

All of the adults laughed, and Grandpa Zeb lifted David up into his arms as he looked at his other grandchildren. "Well, let's just say that I don't think they were ever mean to David again."

Christmas Prayers

Patricia Barrett

The baby would know he was not alone. He would smell my Ralph Lauren perfume. He would hear my songs, he would feel my arms. Together we would step back into our bodies and know the joy, the compassion, and the joy-filled tenderness that life offers a dying soul.

I put water on for tea and forgot. The metallic stench of the kettle burning filtered through the house. I raised the kitchen windows and let the humid heat intrude through the screens. Shortly after, a fireman came, but not because of the burning kettle. I watched the navy uniform with the shiny intimidating badge move noiselessly through my house.

Nervously, I checked the time on the living room clock. Its rich chimes had not poured through the New Hampshire Victorian home. The mantle clock, a centerpiece on the brick fireplace, stood silent, apparently unwound. Coincidently, the battery operated clock hanging on the pantry wall stopped a little before noon. "What on earth is going on?" I thought. "Even the cuckoo clock, my sister's gift from Germany, stopped its tick-tock!" No tugging of the pine-coned chains would start the perpetual tempo to track the hours of a July heat wave.

My husband and I had come home from a weekend camping trip in the White Mountains. On our way up, I was excited for his doctor's visit where he was supposed to receive a prescription for chlomid, an opportunity to increase our 3-year futility in fertility. However, when he left the office, he had decided against taking the fertility drug that might enhance our chances of having a baby. Three longs years of trying had made me an emotional sponge, fixated on my desire to be a mother.

To face the weekend camping trip with friends was only an attempt at normalcy. What was normal? I was a ghost in my own body-a wafting spirit-empty of joy or passion. Dejected, despaired, and drowning in my own pain, I attempted to swallow the sobs that monstrously escaped along the narrow Concord street. "You have a problem! You have to pull it together," he snarled as he walked three steps in front of me. "There are side effects, it's only a 50-50 chance; I don't want to take it, that's all!" An emotional door slammed on my face and I couldn't breathe.

All I really heard him say was, "You have a problem." I believed him. The buildings twirled around. The car ride up the Kancamagus Highway yielded shadows only I could see. Perhaps I participated in the camping trip, but I only felt walls and windows skulking around my soul, and I didn't care if he knew I was crying myself to sleep only when the first robins were announcing everyone's morning bliss…everyone's but mine.

Yet, here was a moment that defied all time. Here was a fireman, right here in my house; he had been called upon to carry out this emergency. The figure checked the water temperature from all of the faucets and peeked into my dishwasher. He scanned the hardwood floors and oriental rugs for small debris. He rattled doors to check locks. All was clean and dust free. Finally, with a grand smile, he left a scribbled report on the dining room table, and, before the navy uniform slipped into the haze of the summer day, he said, "This is for the social worker from DCYS -the Division of Children and Youth Services. Her name is Shaunna, and she will be here with *the baby* in a couple hours."

I floated to the doorway of the spare bedroom, empty for three long years. It loomed with an echo for over thirty-six menstrual cycles and over 12, 040 days of prayers…even novenas. I gazed at old hardwood floors, stained from those who had dwelled before we married and moved in, almost four years ago. The room now had one twin bed, low to the floor, and one white painted bureau, a small detail from my own childhood. Empty tan walls, cleanly painted, looked back at me. No pictures brightened the room, no clothes hung in its closet, and no lamps or stereo invited anyone to visit. The room waited, longing for a baby to bring life to its bleakness and to cure the vast solitude. The room twirled in time; I day-slept back to three years ago.

Snowflakes gathered on the ledge outside my fireplace windows. The greys of the day turned to hues of blue as distant snowplows rumbled up the road. Surround-sound speakers caroled, *"Hark! The Herald Angels Sing!"* Across the mantle I draped festive holly; I wound green wire around a self-made red velvet bow and fastened it to the brass fixture on the Howard Miller, a wedding present mantle clock. It chimed with pride, the classic centerpiece illuminated by white twinkles of light. Beside the candle-lit windows I trimmed the tree with my mom's hand crafted crocheted snowflakes and strategically placed them to highlight sparkling satin bows and shimmering ornaments. I stood back and marveled at the room, a picture right out of some New England gathering room. I placed my hands across my belly and prayed. "Surely there will be a baby next Christmas," God was good and wonderful, I knew. The thought of a newborn by the tree or growing in my womb filled me with joy as I sang my own descant to *"O, Come, All Ye Faithful"*.

I continued trimming the tree with ornaments from a very special box; each ornament, tissue wrapped. For the past five Christmases, the box grew with more ornaments; each treasure, a gift from students in my high school English classes. "Kids, glorious kids!" I said a prayer over each ornament for the generosity of the giver and in gratitude for my profession.

The tree completed, I sat in the Bentwood rocker and felt the beauty of the Christmas season. Soon my husband would be home from work. This man, I loved.

"Do you want a fire?" He asked shaking snow from his boots.

I was delighted. "Yes! Come see the decorations!"

"Beautiful!" He disappeared into the cellar and emerged with a few short logs of oak. Fire kindled and room fragrant, I rocked and rocked.

"Maybe a baby next Christmas, Lord, a baby next Christmas, please?"

The following year was fraught with visits to the infertility clinic. Marital vocabulary and conversations included words like hystersalpingeograms, sperm counts and motility, chlomid, AIH, artificial insemination with husband's sperm, and fertility calendar.

Again, fragrant boughs adorned the mantle and the clock stood proudly gracing the season. The red velvet bow visited with grandeur, and with the clock's quarter hour chime, I prayed as I had the Christmas before, "Maybe a baby next year, Lord, maybe a baby next year." I rocked and let my tears create a white haze of the Christmas tree. The fire crackled and new ornaments joined the old, special prayers said for each, once again. Surely another year would not pass without a baby to grow within…

Throughout the year, I found excuses for not attending friends' baby showers. I hurried by the diaper and baby food aisles, and left the room during Pampers commercials.

"Relax!" My husband said. "There's no rush. We're fine! It'll happen when it happens." We were almost 30, and I doubted if motherhood would ever find my womb. He didn't understand. Something was wrong inside my head and my body. I could feel no pain, but I could feel no joy. I immersed myself in a Master's Degree program and with music at church. I started a youth choir, wrote for publication, developed new curriculum, and kept a basal thermometer by my bed to remind my husband of "It's time for baby-making days".

Alas, Christmas vacation a year later began with a blizzard. Winds whipped the naked maples as the snow slapped at my candle-lit windows. Schools busses came for an early release, and I proudly carried out the new wave of students' Christmas generosity. Baked cookies, balsam candles, #1 teacher ornaments, and other treasures filled my book bag. But, driving through the snow, ready for a two week break, I felt like I was headed for an internal break. A huge lump formed in my throat, and I became angry with God. "No baby again?" I cried aloud in the car. "Why are you so good to others and not me!" It wouldn't have mattered to me if the car found its way into the blinding storm and…I shoved those thoughts aside.

For no apparent reason, we placed the Christmas tree in a different corner of the room this third barren year. Oh, yes, the fireplace mantle and candlelit windows were storybook. The music was soul-filled…I rocked and rocked and felt nothing. Nothing. Nothing. I thought that the tree stared awkwardly at me. At times, I fancied it mocked me. Each ornament, though prayed over, did not offer me the glorious warmth of the seasons before. I shivered in front of the fire and sweat in the open snowy night. Blaring carols did not reach my heart, even my favorite of favorites. I felt large in my slender body and tiny in the queen bed. I rocked and rocked, doubtful and sad. "Maybe a baby next year, Lord, maybe a baby for Christmas next year." I was doubtful. Why did I even keep praying? I thought God abandoned me, and I didn't understand why.

The telephone rang and I jolted from my day sleep. Christmases past flew into the blank tan walls of the sparse spare room, and I jumped. Dizzily, I answered the phone.

"It's me," said my husband. "I'm picking up the crib at my house. It was only used for my sister, and Ma said it's in good shape,"

"Perfect! I like the idea of it staying in the family!"

"It will be awhile. Dad and I have to dig in the attic."

"A social worker called," I said with a bit of fear. "She said they can't leave *the baby* unless we have a crib."

"Don't worry," his voice was reassuring. "We'll get it…Love you…"

I went back to the empty room. Suddenly I saw where the crib would be. I became a whirlwind of creation. I lifted the blue braided rug from the dining room and pulled the Bentwood rocker into the room. "*The baby's* room," I thought with imaginative awe.

An eight week-old baby boy was to be delivered in two hours! The thought of Christmas in July was absurd. I thought of the teen I tutored.

At the beginning of summer she asked me the most painful question I could ever be asked.

"Do you want kids?"

"Yes-yes-I-we-it just hasn't happened."

"Why don't you foster? Most of my brothers and sisters were foster kids."

How could she ask me such a thing. Foster? That was for people who could want, love, and give back…I needed…NEEDED…my own baby. "I don't think I could take a child in only to give up…"

She was matter-of-fact. "They don't all go back. Why do you think I have so many brothers and sisters? I love them just as much as my blood siblings. I don't even know the difference."

Who was teaching whom? Yet, here in this place and time, after an unforgiving weekend in the mountains, her mother had called while I was crying and fretting over my husband's chlomid decision.

"Did you know I'm a foster home-finder? Let me tell you about *this emergency*. Are you sitting down? He's an 8 week-old failure-to-thrive. He spent two weeks going through drug and alcohol withdrawal…Crack. Cocaine…Unfortunately, he was allowed to go home to biological mother. She left him alone…48 hours or more…crying…abandoned…needs bonding…needs to be placed today…emergency…not crying for basic needs 8 lbs. 4 oz.…neglected baby boy…foster with intent to adopt…was taken Friday…emergency foster home….needs real foster home…"

The officials came to pick up *the baby* at the same time the streets in Concord were caving in on me while I followed behind my husband like a lost, forlorn puppy. *The baby* was transported to an emergency foster home while Kancamagus Highway shadows tangled my vision of the Old Man in the Mountain. *The baby* slept in a strange crib while I, in a tent, stifled cries, imploding from my own un-nurtured need to be a mother.

I placed a portable stereo on the bureau and set the radio for Mozart and Bach to visit the room. *The baby* would know he was not alone. He would smell my Ralph Lauren perfume. He would hear my songs, he would feel my arms. Together we would step back into our bodies and know the joy, the compassion, and the joy-filled tenderness that life offers a dying soul

I giggled at my own sense of humor and sang, "*Hark! The Herald Angels Sing.*" At that moment, a definite breeze passed through my hair; it brushed my right arm and slender leg. No curtains waved. No leaf fluttered. Was it my imagination? New Hampshire homes rarely had air conditioning, and mine was one. The breeze circled my sandaled toes. I ventured to the large windowed dining room where I could see several maples and oaks. Still the breeze breathed throughout the house-"Not a creature was stirring, not even a mouse." Outside, the muggy humidity sat on the still leaves. Like a buzzard, the heat perched on the green tresses and arching limbs throughout the neighborhood, but inside my house, the reminder of living air danced around me. I looked at the clock, still stopped at 10:45. "Is that when the foster home-finder called me?" I wondered. . .

I called Mimi, my close friend; I would have to wait for Trish to get home from work. They listened incredulously. "We're getting a baby! IN A COUPLE HOURS! A home-finder for foster care knew of us and called. A failure-to-thrive 8 week-old infant boy needs bonding immediately. Parental rights are in the process of termination, so we'll foster with the intent of adoption!"

"Oh, my God, Oh, my GOD, Oh, my GAWD! What do you need?" she asked.

I was stunned. I hadn't thought of that. "I don't know! What do I need!" For the first time my stomach tilted with excitement. This was real. Diapers. Bottles. Formula. Crib sheets. Powder. What else? I had been obnoxiously absent at the entourage of baby showers. I promised myself I would never miss another baby shower.

The doorbell rang before my husband was home with the crib. Shaunna, a sweet Irish-looking woman in her twenties, stood, and cradled in one arm, an infant the size of a newborn! In her other hand, she held a brown paper bag containing a couple bottles, a couple diapers, and an outfit. That was all he had to *his name*.

Time stood still for me at this moment. With full smile and giving nature, Shaunna shifted the sleeping baby boy into my arms.

I really didn't know how to hold a baby. As we walked inside, she gently showed me how to hold his weak, tiny head. I couldn't take my eyes off of him. Sleeping, his eyelashes drifted down to his cheeks. His dark skin revealed weeks of neglect and abandonment, for it was easy to see muscle tissue behind the white skin. He had five tiny toes on each foot and five tiny fingers on each hand, fingernails fully formed and sharp. His full lips were pursed into a pout, but when he opened his eyes…Lord, when he opened his eyes…his soul saw mine.

"You can call him by any name if you want," Shaunna warned, "but he still must go by his legal name for all records. When the adoption is complete, then he will receive a new social security number, new birth certificate, and all old records of his birth except for medical reasons will be sealed. That means no one will be able to come after him or find him for any reason. His life has been endangered, and it is law that he must be kept safe."

"Jj. We will call him Jj until his adoption is final. Then his name will be Joseph, after my father and after my husband's grandfather."

The crib came. The friends came with crib bumpers and blankets and diapers and bathtub and bottles and….grateful, I certainly was, but I couldn't take my eyes off my son. MY SON.

The social workers counseled me to be careful, that I was a "foster mother" even though the case would "most likely" conclude in termination of biological parental rights. This could take up to year, perhaps more. Still, we would bond. We would attach. With adoption, he would be Joseph Patrick, the son of my soul.

"Trish? I called my life-long friend. "Are you sitting down?"

"Sitting? Yes." I knew she wasn't.

"Really? I have something to tell you. We *have* a baby!"

Jj's biological mother accepted one visit three weeks later. Shaunna came to pick him up and bring him for a supervised visit at the DCYS. She invited me to come watch through a two-way mirror, but I did not want any memory or knowledge of the biological mother in my brain. I harbored anger at the 34 year-old woman; I was not angry at her drug addiction and the newborn state she put the baby in. I was not angry that she didn't really want him, anyway. I was not angry that he had a two-and-a-half year-old brother whose whereabouts were unknown. I was angry at her for being able to have a baby and deliberately leaving him alone, un-diapered, unfed, untouched; I was angry at her for being able to have a baby and creating a silent prison in a world he could not comprehend. I was angry at her for being able to have a baby and making the tiny innocent soul lose the will to live. I was angry at her for being able to have a baby and intending to sell "it" for drug money. I was angry at her for being able to have a baby when I could not. I had a son without being able to breast feed. Foster care would not allow it, anyway. I had a son without being able to share labor stories. I had a son without having a baby shower. She would never know the extent of my anger infused with obvious envy, that God allowed people like her to have babies, and why not me? No. I wanted her to disappear and thanked the angels who brought my son to me for his life for giving him the struggle to survive.

When Shaunna and Jj left, I felt what a mother owl must feel when she cannot find her owlet. I paced. I prayed. I put the teakettle on and forgot. I imagined the worse. "She" would have a piece of paper from the judge allowing her to take the baby back. "She" would be in AA, parent project, born-again, and other lovely programs showing her to be a fit mother. "She" would steal the baby, run out the back door into a waiting car, and disappear. That was actually the most plausible, and I put myself into a panic. I relived information I had learned about my son's life: the plan for the baby was to be on a bus to New York where he would be sold to Jewish attorneys who would adopt him out for $25,000. "Her" cut would be $5,000. The plan was shut down by his own biological grandfather, "her" father, who said the baby's life was in danger, and he would testify. Social services took the baby to the emergency foster home that day… the day the streets in Concord twisted and twirled. The grandfather died the next day. That day I had gone off into the woods where no one would see me or hear me; I cried. Now I cried for the grandfather whose last good deed on earth changed two destinies, his grandchild's and a woman whom he would never know-a woman who couldn't have a baby.

I paced. I looked at the bottles of formula I made. I marveled at how the color of Enfamil was the color of his room. I shoved aside the idea of looking at his empty crib. Was I so accustomed to tortuous thoughts that I brought them on myself? I looked at the pantry clock, ticking with its new battery. Suddenly, the doorbell rang, and I jumped.

There in the front door window was Shaunna and a red-faced wailing son. Shaunna was laughing as I opened the door and immediately reached for Jj. "Hey, there," I cooed. "What's all this, Handsome thing?" I cradled and waltzed the now 11 week 11 lb. baby.

Jj opened his eye between wails and began to sputter, still red-faced and sweaty. I swayed back and forth and chattered…"It's okay…what are you thinking? You didn't like the car ride? Did you go on an adventure? Did you go visiting? Did you know I missed you? Did you know I put that teakettle on and forgot again? Did you know how very much I missed you?"   Shaunna watched and listened. Jj stopped snorting and sputtering, and took a stuttering gasp of air every few moments while he looked up at me. I shifted him from my cradled arms and balanced him on one breast so his tiny sweaty cheek nestled into my neck. I rubbed his back, his silky curls, and let his bottom balance on my forearm.

Still Shaunna watched and listened though I had temporarily forgotten about her. Jj and I walked to the refrigerator. "Do you want a bottle? Bottle?" I enunciated. We swayed through the kitchen and rocked while I heated the bottle. Gently, gradually, his chaotic gasps and snorts dwindled to calm alertness. Still slow to eat, an hour for a mere 4 ounces, Jj took the bottle and startled himself when intermittent post-sobbing blasts of air shook him from belly to throat.

"He's bonded," Shaunna nodded proudly.

"He has?" I asked like a child hoping for a gold star on a project. Jj WAS my project, my mission, my purpose.

"Oh, yes. He started a bit when we left. "She" was late, and just when we thought she wouldn't show up, she did. She wreaked of cigarette smoke, and as soon as she held him, he started up big time….Big time," Shaunna expected me to understand what she was really saying, but I was caught in my own web of jealousy and didn't notice her raised eyebrows when she described Jj's unpleasant communicative behavior. "When he didn't settle, and she couldn't get him settled, she cut her meeting short and left." I nodded acknowledging I had heard her though Jj and I were looking at each other as he sucked the formula.

"I took him around a bit, but he didn't settle for me either. But this? I have to write a report about this," Shaunna said referring to Jj and me. "Once he was back here with you, hearing you, seeing you, this is bonding. Only someone he's attached to could get him out of that kind of separation anxiety. This report will help toward the termination of parental rights and fostering with the intent to adopt. It's just a matter of time now. If she skips her next appointment, the finding for abandonment begins today."

In the months between my son's "Christmas in July Homecoming" and the December Christmas season, my prayers revealed God's abiding love for all of us. At first, Jj never cried, not for food, not for diapering, and certainly not for attention; how could he want what he never had? Soft whimpers upon his awakening sent me joyfully to his crib. During the day, he often slept in a snuggly, a front pack where his tiny head rested on my breasts. There, he could move with me, hear me, and feel me so I could heal the void from the quiet abandonment of his first weeks of life. At the foot of his crib, I placed a clean flannel nightgown sprayed lightly with Ralph Lauren perfume, my fragrant reminder that his new mother was ever-present, nearby and attached.

He grew slowly but steadily. Wide-eyed and serious, he studied my face until he nodded off in my arms. We bonded as I fed him close to the warmth of my breast and near my beating heart. His room became a Testament of answered prayers. Royal blue curtains blew freely in the breeze as birds' songs met the Tree of Life, a Navajo woven bright tapestry dawned on a wall in his room. Big Bird, Bert and Ernie, and other Sesame Street characters in a mobile carousel, turned and chimed over his crib.

Jj was 7 months-old in front of the adorned Christmas tree that held his fascination, and I moved the rocker out of his room to the festive living room where I could rock him and rock him, and sing, "Hark! The Herald Angels Sing…Glory to the newborn King!"

"You sent me my baby this Christmas, Lord, you sent me a baby this year!" I rocked and rocked. Not yet adopted, he was a thriving seven month old struggling to sit up by himself. Santa's visit brought a jolly jumper and teething rings, cool dude jeans with snaps for easy diapering, and a baby pack for his dad's back.

It took two following Christmases for the sacred celebration of Christ's love and answered prayers. Though Jj's leaving me was an obscure threat, the legal processes of terminating parents' rights was painfully arduous. I fought for my son's adoption when files were lost and procedures needed to begin again. I just followed my attorney-dad's advice: write a letter to the governor and Cc: everyone in the up-line of DCYS. It worked. We signed adoption papers three days before Christmas. Jj was 2 ½ years old. Hadn't three clocks stopped so long ago, the day he arrived? Had our angels actually united us and danced with us lest we ever wondered if prayers would be answered?

Joseph Patrick Barrett was then baptized on the evening before Christmas Eve, with close friends and family witnessing our family miracle. We gathered at the house after church for New England seafood chowder and seasoned eggnog. The tree stood like a regal king in its favorite corner. I fancied it honored me. White lights were diamond gems, stars of the Christmastide. I rocked and rocked and glowed like the velvet bow on the clock as it chimed. My prayers were answered. I became a mother in three hours, the day three clocks stopped all on the same day…and the cuckoo clock? It never did 'cuckoo' again. Actually, I never felt 'cuckoo' again either.

The fire crackled, I sang descants and harmonies to every carol while *my son* played and listened, and he told us what he wanted from Santa. It was simple. "A hamma' and some tooooools."

Seven and a half years later, Christmas prayers and angels' dances were celebrated once again. Joe was now not only our son, he was now Leah Marirose's big brother. After ten years, the other prayers got answered: I gave birth to a daughter. Clocks didn't stop this time; time just stopped to answer prayers.

Autumn Heart

John Newlin

I own an autumn heart,
a pumpkin ripened by time,
subliminally carved,
regret's candle burning within.

I harvest the fruits of love
in lemon crates
on a wagon pulled by
a gored ox.

Wobbling in the ruts,
past yesterday's castles,
past frosted fields
of sterile grain.

Past straw sentries,
grinning effigies,
watching the crows
through sightless eyes.

Rumbling over wood decking
creaking in protest,
a grating warning that it is
the bridge of no return.

Autumn's music reigns,
plaintive refrains
vibrating in veinless leaves
destined soon to fall.

Cowled winter awaits,
its frosty greeting
crisp and certain
in its cold, cruel finality.

Author Bios

Aiswarya T. Anish is 14 years old, lives in a small village in India, and has written poetry since she was 3. She has written more than 400 poems and 3 novels in two languages. She recently released a book of poetry entitled "A Crescent Smile." She has performed several readings and interviews for Asia Net Television. Her interests include philosophy and reading and has a strong love for world peace, which is decreasing in our world day by day. Her village in Kerala was destroyed by the great Tsunami of 2004, but has managed to rebuild and be happy in their lives.

Lisa Arnold is an accomplished freelance writer, published poet, and short story author who has been writing poems and short stories for nearly three decades. Her work has appeared in several issues of "All Things Girl", "Events Quarterly", "Poetic Monthly, "Good Taste International", "The Persistent Mirage", "Rewind the Fifties", "Yo Naturals" and "Southport Times." She is also the founder and administrator of a growing online poetry community called *Echoes of My Soul Poetry Forum*, and she was a staff writer for *Poetic Monthly*. She resides in Ohio.

Mary Barnet's first book, "The New American/Selected Poems," followed four chapbooks, including "Orchidia" and "Landscape." She was the Featured Writer in a special edition of *Poet* magazine. Her poetry has appeared in "Crossroads", "Gusto", "New Worlds Unlimited", "The New Jersey Poetry Society Anthology", "Funky Dog Publishing", "Recursive Angel", "The Greenwich Village Gazette", "The Poem Factory", "Numbat", "The Pittsburgh Review", and elsewhere. She is founder and chief editor of *PoetryMagazine.com* and produces poetry films with Richard E. Schiff. Her latest book of poetry is entitled "Arrival". MS Barnet is a 2010 Nobel Peace Prize nominee. She is the wife of artist, social activist & filmmaker Richard E. Schiff. Mary is the daughter of artist Mary Sinclair and painter Will Barnet.

Patricia Barrett is an English teacher and Department chair at Sacramento's Foothill High School. She has contributed numerous articles to the *Sacramento Bee* and *Placer Herald*. Most recently, Patricia was featured in "Chicken Soup for the New Mother." She resides in Foresthill, California and has launched a new poetic genre, which she calls MAG Poetry, *Mothers Against Gangs*, where she uses her insight and experiences to enlighten readers on the bittersweet perspective of those whose lives are touched by gang activity.

Erin Brennan is a sixth grade student, and is eleven years old. Erin lives in Albuquerque, New Mexico and is a gifted student who attends McKinley Middle school. She won the spelling bee for her school in 2010 and likes to sculpt in clay. Her artwork can be seen on the JB Stillwater website. Erin loves all animals, writing, swimming and arts.

Janet K. Brennan, aka J. B. Stillwater, is a novelist, poet, publisher and book critic. She wrote her first novel "Teristen" at the age of 12. Her short stories and poetry have been published around the world, most recently, "SP Quill Magazine", "Common Swords Magazine", "The Power of Prayerful Living", and "Prevention Magazine." She was a contributor to "Chicken Soup for the Soul", "Chicken Soup for the Christmas Soul 2008", "Chicken Soup for the Traveler's Soul", and "Chicken Soup for the Positive Thinker." She contributed articles for "Taj Mahal Review" and "Different Worlds, a Virtual Journey." Her colored pencil artwork and photography have been published in both the United States and Europe. She has contributed short stories, poetry and philosophical essays to *Strangeroad.com* as well as *IdentityTheory.com.* Her contributions include "Existentialism; a Myopic View." She has written three books of poetry, "Recollections of an Old Mind, West",

"A Stronger Grace", and "Gentle Tugs," as well as two novels, "A Dance in the Woods" and "Harriet Murphy: A Little Bit of Something." Janet has edited and contributed to "Holiday Word Gifts" which will be released in 2011, and is currently working on her next novel, "Judas Chant." Janet's work is featured in New Mexico Book Award finalist "Earthships: A New Mecca", and was a featured poet on Mary Barnet's "The Poetry Magazine." Janet attended the University of New Hampshire and Hesser Business College and holds a legal certificate from the University of New Mexico.

Tracey Brown's 54 years on this earth had no real significance until November 11, 2003. That was the day she was arrested and spent 17 months in the Richland Parish Detention Center in Rayville, Louisiana. With the help of a dear friend, she completed her Masters and Ph.D. in Business Administration. Afterwards, she taught at a number of schools before opening her own consulting business. She has released a book "I Found my Father in a women's Prison" and a travels the country performing plays and lectures with her "Reach Out in Hope Ministry."

Michelle D'Ambrosio was born in Philadelphia and started writing poetry in fifth grade. She has a B.S. in Psychology and a Bachelor of Divinity from St. Joseph's University. Upon graduation, she started a natural foods company called "Michele's Original," which flourished for 25 years before moving to Sarasota, Fla. She published her first book of poetry "The Four Corners" with a local photographer, Jan Michael, in May 2009. "The 12 Commitments" will be released in 2012. She was married to the world-renowned artist, Pepe Rovira and is working as a Life Coach.

Peggie Devan is a poet and is currently writing a series of children's books, entitled "Bella's Early Bloomers, by Boo and Gap." She has a Baccalaureate in psychology and is a registered nurse. She is a guest poet in Janet K. Brennan's book "Gentle Tugs: a Celebration of Life, Love and Other Addictions." She was the winner of the Josh Groban poetry contest in 2007.

Lola R. Eagle is an author, free-lance writer, and poet living in Albuquerque, New Mexico. She has written two books of poetry: "From the Eye of an Eagle" and "More Visions in Verse." Her poetry has appeared in many national and local magazines and newspapers, as well as several hardcover anthologies. A member of Southwest Writers, she is twice widowed and resides with her faithful canine companion, Lucy.

Frances Fanning has been a writer and a poet all her life, filling copybooks and journals with her rhythms and musings since she was a young girl. A trained marriage, family, and drug and alcohol therapist, Frances has worked in business, journalism and the arts, as owner/operator of a contemporary American craft gallery in an art colony in Pennsylvania.

Charles Adès Fishman created the Visiting Writers Program at Farmingdale State College in 1979 and served as director until 1997. He also developed the Distinguished Speakers Program for Farmingdale State and led that program from 2001 through 2007. In addition, he was cofounder of the *Long Island Poetry Collective*, a founding editor of *Xanadu* magazine and *Pleasure Dome Press*, and originated the *Paumanok Poetry Award Competition*. He was editor of the Water Mark Poets of North America Book Award (1980-83), associate editor of *The Drunken Boat*, and poetry editor of *Gaia, Cistercian Studies Quarterly*, the *Journal of Genocide Studies*, and *New Works Review*, and is poetry editor of *Prism: An Interdisciplinary Journal For Holocaust Educators* and consultant in poetry to the U.S. Holocaust Memorial Museum in Washington, D.C. Among Fishman's most recent awards and honors are the Walt Whitman Birthplace Association's *Long Island Poet of the Year* and the 2007 Paterson Award for Literary Excellence. His books include *Mortal Companions, The Death Mazurka*, an American Library Association Outstanding Book of the Year that was nominated for the 1990 Pulitzer Prize in Poetry, and *Blood to Remember: American Poets on the Holocaust*

Terri French originally hails from Michigan, but has lived in northern Alabama for 20 years. She has a degree in journalism and is a licensed massage therapist. She spent time as a freelance writer for several local newspapers, in library reference, and as a barista. She devotes her time to writing, yoga, long walks, cooking, and a good glass of cabernet or zinfandel (not the pink stuff!).

Katrina K Guarascio is a poet from Albuquerque, New Mexico. She has authored two books of poetry "A Scattering of Imperfections" and "They don't make memories like that anymore..." She written several chapbooks, serves on poetry judging boards around the country, and is a slam poetry performer. She recently toured the United States with the "Off the Page and On a Tangent" tour.

Michelle Hed is a photographer, poet, and artist living in Minnesota. Her poems have appeared in the following books and online journals: *A Handful of Stones, Pay Attention: A River of Stones, Haiga Online*, and was a finalist in the *Poetic Asides Poem a Day Challenge 2009*. Her photography has won awards and appeared in *Minnesota Birding*. She also penned a book, "*Natural Musings*," which contains both her photography and poetry. She maintains a blog, *The Pen, Lens and Brush,* is married to her best friend, and has two beautiful daughters and two mischievous hounds.

Lee Hepworth. is an author and poet who lives in the U.K. His writing style is that of the early scholars, Milton and Dante. He publishes his work on Echoes of My Soul Poetry, as well as JB Stillwater Literary Magazine

Granville Holt is a poet of Cherokee heritage and hails from the great state of Oklahoma. He is the guest author in Janet Brennan's, "Recollections of an Old mind, West" Granville Holt also writes for several poetry publications such as "Echoes of the Soul" and "The Poet Sanctuary"

Jon Hovis is a Western fiction writer from the state of Maryland, currently living in the desert of New Mexico. He is an associate member of the Western Writers of America, an organization which promotes the literature and authors of the American West. Jon has written three books, "The Feather Gang", "The Preacher", and "Silverton Gold." His latest novel "Anasazi Ruin" will be released in 2012

D. Allen Jenkins, from the lovely state of Ohio, is a writer and poet, published Winter 2004 in "The Private Lantern," and in Shadows of the Season; The Member's Collection- 2004." Released in the spring of 2005, a novel, "The Making of Tibias Ivory: Freedom's Quest" and "The Making of Tibias Ivory: Through the Eyes of Innocence."

Kairawan Joseph is a poet residing in Sarasota, Florida, where she is a medical assistant for a physician's office. She is a lover of creative writing and literature in many forms. Kairawan began writing poetry after her daughter (and only child) started college last fall. Since then, poetry has become a favorite pastime and passion. Her poetry is often whimsical and touches on many aspects of life.

Santosh Kumar. is a poet, short-story writer, and editor from India. He has a Doctorate of Philosophy in English, and is the Dean of Literature at Allahabad University in India. He is the editor of "Taj Mahal Review" and "Harvests of New Millennium" and has written numerous books of poetry, including "Helicon" and "No Nukes: Brave New World." Dr. Kumar has presented papers which include *Words: One Path to Peace and Understanding* which was presented at the Oslo Norway literary festival in 2008, *The Fabric of Vision, The Still Horizon, Indian Verse, The Golden Wings, Voyages, Symphonies*, and *New Pegasus*. He is the Dean of Literature at Allahabad University, India

Jill Lane is a magazine travel writer and New Mexico tourism specialist. In 2004, she founded Enchantment

Lane Publications, a New Mexico based boutique-publishing house focusing on children's books. The company's aim is to provide quality activity books with an educational message. Her books introduce children to real places and things in New Mexico. "New Mexico A to Z" won the 2008 New Mexico Book Award in the "Best Children's Activity Book" category, and "Hello Cinder Bear!" was named a finalist. Her newest book, "OsoBear's Spanish-English Primer" was also a finalist in 2010 and has had great success in the bilingual arena including an orphanage in Mexico. She and her dog, Travelin' Jack, visit and report on pet-cations around New Mexico and they donate proceeds from some of their books to support local animal welfare organizations in New Mexico.

Katherine Luke is an artist living in New Mexico. Kate attended the University of New Mexico and is founder of Abstract Wizardries and Design, Albuquerque, New Mexico. She is the mother of Erin Elizabeth, who was diagnosed with Leukemia at the age of five. Erin is now in remission and expects to have her last chemo treatment in October of 2007 Kate is also the mothrof Peyton Alexander, age 7 and Nathan Joseph, age 5.

Robert Mirabal, nicknamed Toop-yah-oh (Flute Song) in his Native American Tiwa language, hails from the Taos Pueblo in northern New Mexico. He is a multitalented instrumentalist who crafts his own flutes. He writes poetry, prose, and screenplays and developed a musical style that has been billed as "alter-Native" music. Robert completed a run on Broadway in Peter Buffet's "Spirit--A Journey in Dance, Drum, and Song." In 2001, he released "Music from a Painted Cave," a live concert recorded at the Fox Theater in Mashantucket, Connecticut. His short story collection, "Skeleton of a Bridge," was published in 1995. His flutes are on display at the Smithsonian Institute in Washington, D.C., and his artwork was included in "Native American Artists of North America." Mirabal's writings were used by Robert Redford to compile the documentaries "Silent Witness and Sacred Sites." A respected composer, Mirabal's works have been performed at the John F. Kennedy Center for the Performing Arts and at the Brooklyn Academy of Music.

John Newlin lives in San Diego, California and is an award winning photographer and poet. He has penned a book of poetry entitled "The Poetry Café" and has done book cover designs. During his 23-year career in the Navy, he flew fighter jets from the decks of 11 different aircraft carriers in the Pacific and Atlantic Oceans and the Mediterranean Sea and saw aerial combat in the skies over North Vietnam. He has a Bachelor of Arts in mathematics from San Diego State University and a Bachelor of Science in Computer Science.

Mia Alexandra Oelnes is a mum of two boys, aged 3 and 7. She lives in Oslo, Norway with her husband. She has a bachelor of Nursing Studies from Oslo University College, and is now studying to become a librarian. Her hobbies are, among others, photography with a special interest in macrophotography. Wild flowers are her favorite subjects.

Rainer Ochs Pasca, 5, lives in New York with his parents and little brother Atticus. He enjoys learning Spanish and ASL, swimming in hotel pools, and is excited about mostly everything, especially people. He loves traveling and has been to 28 states, Canada and Spain. As a Kindergartener, Rainer was awarded the Town of Islip Achievement Award for excellence in Social Studies and he has self-published a small book of his poems entitled "Rooftops and War." Two of Rainer's poems are set to appear in the fall 2011 issue of "The Louisville Review," and he is currently working on a second volume of work entitled "In the Night".

Kathryn Rantala's fiction and poetry have appeared in "Denver Quarterly", "Field", "Iowa Review", "Archipelago", and "Painted Bride Quarterly." She is the author of "Traveling With the Primates", "The Plant Waterer and Other Things in Common", "Missing Pieces: a Coroner's Companion" and "A Partial View Toward Nazareth." She is the founder of Ravenna Press.

Patricia Saunders is president of a non-profit organization, Medford Arts Center, Inc., and a photographer specializing in scenes from around New England. In 2005 Patricia published a local history book "Medford: Then and Now" including historic photos of Medford's past and present. Patricia makes her home in Boston, MA.

Richard E. Schiff is a life member of the Art Students League of New York and began his studies there in 1963. "Fine Arts Magazine Spring 2009" featured his article on Will Barnet, one of his teachers. Schiff's work has been exhibited internationally in many collections in the U.S. and abroad, and his work is in the Jerusalem Museum of Fine Arts by the 1991 painting "Homeless." Richard Schiff makes his home in Toms River, New Jersey. He is the editor-in-chief and founder of the *Greenwich Village Gazette*, a NYC publication.

Andrew Shiston was born on the Island of Portland in Dorset. At fifteen, he joined the Merchant Navy and sailed on passenger liners and many other vessels, including the large crude carriers. Captain Shiston is listed in the "Guinness Book of Records" for having logged in the most hours at sea. He has authored two books of poetry and a novel entitled "Memoirs of a Merchant Marine."

R.J. Slais is a poet living in Romeo, Michigan. As an inventor and engineer for a metro Detroit automotive industry supplier, he has ten U.S. patents. He is a former magazine editor and artist and has written for such magazines as "Barnwood Poetry Magazine", "Boston Literary Magazine", "MiPOesias", "Pedestal Magazine", and "Rose and Thorn Journal." RJ recently finished a chapbook entitled "Mice Verses Man."

Lynn Strongin resides in British Columbia, Canada. She contracted polio at the age of twelve. She graduated from Hunter College cum laude and, having won a Woodrow Wilson Fellowship, went to Stanford University where she obtained an M.A. Strongin taught at various post-secondary institutions in New York State and California and moved to Albuquerque to start her Doctoral studies at the University of New Mexico. She received a National Endowment of the Arts (NEA) Creative Writing grant and penned, "The Dwarf Cycle." Lynn has authored eight books of poetry and was nominated for a Pulitzer Prize for her book, "Spectral Freedom."

Katriona Wallace is a poet who was raised in Stirling, Scotland, moved to Norway where she now lives, and works as senior purchaser for a French metal producing company. She writes nature poetry as a hobby.

Florence Weinberg has traveled to Canada, Germany, France, and Spain. After earning her PhD, she taught at St. John Fisher College in Rochester, NY and Trinity University in San Antonio. She published four scholarly books, many articles and book reviews, doing research in the U.S. and abroad. Florence has produced ten novels, ranging from fantasy to historical romance and mystery, which have been translated into French, and three historical mysteries starring the 18th-century Jesuit missionary, Father Ignaz (Ygnacio) Pfefferkorn. Two of these are set in the Sonoran Desert, the third in an ancient monastery in Spain. The book in press is a further Pfefferkorn mystery that follows his fate after his release from Spanish prison: "Unrest in Eden." Four of the historical novels have received a total of eight awards, some of them multiple: "Apache Lance: Franciscan Cross" (three awards), about the founding of San Antonio, "Seven Cities of Mud" (one award), Florence has just completed her last Pfefferkorn mystery which is being translated into German and Spanish.

Sarah Wilson is an award winning Appalachian born writer who has a young soul that clings to green peaks, and a passion that loves the language of words. Long toenails dig deep in mountain soil to unearth goals and promises made to herself. Author Wilson is a storyteller of both the fabulous and the mundane. She has over twenty-eight publications and one Christian book to her credit. Poetry and children works are among her favorites. Her mother (who is an avid genealogist) tells her she is related to Daniel Boone, Jim Bowie, and President

Janet Yaeger lives with her husband in southern Illinois and is a mother of identical twin daughters and a son. She writes poetry about real life situations and considers herself part poet, part storyteller. She has been published in a regional periodical and is a regular contributor at The Poet Sanctuary. Jan Yaeger is guest poet in Janet K. Brennan's book "Gentle Tugs" and is about to release a children's book "Matilda's Upside-down Smile."

David Lester Young was born in Akron, Ohio and lived in South America and Europe for a short period of time. He then graduated into the Vietnam conflict. He started writing *napkin poetry* that always questions. David Young's work can be read on many on line publications, most recently "Echoes of the Soul"

Index

A

Anish, Aiswarya T.
    Bio, 103
    Festival Day, 82
Arnold, Lisa
    Bio, 103
    Christmas Morning, 72

B

Barnet, Mary
    Bio, 103
    Lamb, 55
Barrett, Patricia
    Bio, 103
    Christmas Prayers, 94
Brennan, Art
    San Felipe de Neri Church, 66
Brennan, Erin
    Bio, 103
    The Power of Christmas, 5
Brennan, Janet K.
    A Christmas Prayer, 37
    A Rose in Winter, 65
    Bio, 103
    Dusting Cobwebs on a Winter Day, 7
    Friends of Montecchia, 8
    Gracie's Dream, 66
    Kirche im Algau, 61
    Margaret's Painted Horse, 33
    Misty Morn on Old Gray Pond, 31
    On Any Given Christmas, 11
    Silent Night on the Mountain, 6
    Spirits, 26
    The Christmas Tassel, 3
    The Holiday Ride, 48
    The Last Hunt, 22
    The Little Shop on Piazza Erbe, 18
    The Twelve Days of Christmas, 38
Brown, Tracey
    Bio, 104
    May God Bless You, 74

D

D'Ambrosio, Michelle
    Bio, 104
    Earth Kisses, 4

Devan, Peggie
    Bio, 104
    Snowy Island, 62

E

Eagle, Lola R.
    A Family Tradition, 88
    Bio, 104
    HalloGivingMas, 87
    Please Santa, Give ME a Break!, 89
    Too Much Snow, 86

F

Fanning, Frances
    Bio, 104
    Christmas in New Mexico, 71
Fishman, Charles Adès
    A Chanukah Song, 67
    At Winter Solstice, 47
    Bio, 104
French, Terri
    Bio, 105
    Haiku, 80
    Spruce, 80
    The Fire Burns, 61

G

Guarascio, Katrina K
    A Christmas Eve Proposition, 76
    Bio, 105
    Winter Tree, 75

H

Hed, Michelle
    Bio, 105
    Haiku, 80
Hepworth, Lee
    Bio, 105
    Untitled, 70
Holt, Granville
    Bio, 105
    We are Tsa la gi, 25
Hovis, Jon
    Bio, 105
    Old Maude, 83

J

Jenkins, D. Allen
    Bio, 105
    Never Alone, 90
Joseph, Kairawan
    Bio, 105
    Time, 78

K

Kumar, Santosh
    Bio, 105
    The Jesus I Knew, 56

L

Lane, Jill
    Bio, 105
    The Christmas Train, 58
Luke, Katherine
    Bio, 106
    Calalilly, 64

M

Mirabal, Robert
    Bio, 106
    Christmas Eve, 45

N

Newlin, John
    Autumn Heart, 101
    Bio, 106

O

Oelnes, Mia Alexandra
    Bio, 106
    Ice Cabin, 63
    Ice Trees, 63

P

Pasca, Rainer Ochs
    Bio, 106
    Rooftops and War, 10

R

Rantala, Kathryn
    Bio, 106
    The Christmas Moon, 51

S

Saunders, Patricia
    Bio, 106
    Holiday Tree, 65
    Wreaths, 62
Schiff, Richard E.
    Bio, 107
    Nativity, 64
Shiston, Andrew
    Bio, 107
    Portland, Isle of Slingers, 79
Slais, R.J.
    Bio, 107
    Christmas Mountain, 53
Strongin, Lynn
    Bio, 107
    Christmas in the Last Century, 69

W

Wallace, Katriona
    Bio, 107
    December Morning, 73
Weinberg, Florence
    Bio, 107
    Joanna and the Magi, 40
Wilson, Sarah
    Angels Among Us, 16
    Bio, 107

Y

Yaeger, Janet
    Bio, 108
    Christmas Glow, 68
Young, David Lester
    Bio, 108
    Reflective Christmas Ornaments, 52